WILD HEART
WILD HEART MOUNTAIN: WILD RIDERS MC
BOOK SIX

SADIE KING

WILD HEART

She's off-limits and half his age, but this ex-military biker is a protector hero who won't give up the woman who captures his heart.

Isabella Berone has haunted my dreams since I watched her strut into the White Out nightclub two years ago.

She was too young then, the mafia princess with something to prove. But I watched, and I waited.

When Isabella needs me, I'm there for her. I'll protect her with my life. Because despite the age gap, despite her being off limits, I've fallen for the wild mafia princess.

When her father comes for her, I'll be ready. I swore to fight for my country once, and now I'll fight for Isabella, no matter the cost.

Wild Heart is a protector hero, forbidden love, age gap romance featuring the President of an MC and the wild and curvy mafia princess who steals his heart.

Copyright © 2023 by Sadie King.

All rights reserved.

No part of this book may be reproduced in any form or by any electronic or mechanical means, including information storage and retrieval systems, without written permission from the author, except for the use of brief quotations in a book review.

Cover designed by Cormer Covers.

This is a work of fiction. Any resemblance to actual events, companies, locales or persons living or dead, are entirely coincidental.

Please respect the author's hard work and do the right thing.

www.authorsadieking.com

CONTENTS

1. Raiden — 1
2. Isabella — 9
3. Raiden — 16
4. Isabella — 27
5. Raiden — 40
6. Isabella — 49
7. Raiden — 57
8. Isabella — 66
9. Raiden — 75
10. Isabella — 81
11. Raiden — 91
12. Raiden — 99
13. Isabella — 107
14. Raiden — 113
15. Isabella — 120
    Epilogue — 127

Bonus Scene — 135
Wild Valentine — 139
Books and Series by Sadie King — 151
About the Author — 153

1
RAIDEN

The air is thick with expensive cologne and the smell of fruity cocktails. Pop music blasts from the speakers near the dance floor, making me want to cover my ears and high tail it out of here.

Coming to the White Out isn't my idea of a good time, but it's not every day one of my MC gets married, although it's happening more and more these days. Arlo's in his early thirties and not an old man like me, so when White Out, the club at the Emerald Heart Resort, was suggested for his bachelor party, I agreed that I'd come and not complain about the music.

That was before I got here.

The beat goes way too fast to be comfortable and the lyrics are shouted rather than sung, making me question the musical ability of the vocalist. Why the hell they can't put on something decent that everyone loves, like Foo Fighters, I don't know. Hell, I'd even go for classic pop. Give me Duran Duran and Madonna over this shit any day.

"Here you go." The bartender slides a tray of shot glasses filled with white liquid at me. I squint at the tray, trying to understand why I've got a tray of tequila shots in front of me.

"I didn't order these."

The bartender smiles nervously, and a bead of sweat glistens on his forehead.

We're not wearing our cuts tonight out of respect to Axel. He's the owner of this joint, and I don't want to bring him any trouble. Not that my boys are trouble. But I've come across the type of entitled hot heads who frequent the Emerald Heart Resort, and an MC patch can attract the wrong kind of attention from those kinds of dickheads.

But even without the jackets, we're pretty imposing. My guys are all ex-military and built for strength. Half the MC have beards and tattoos that dress shirts won't fully cover. Compared to the scrawny rich kids on the dance floor, we stand out. Axel would have clocked us the moment we walked in and no doubt let his staff know the Wild Riders Motorcycle Club are in tonight.

"That guy ordered them..." The bartender licks his lips nervously. "...and he said you were paying." His head tilts to the left, indicating someone further down the bar.

I lean forward to see past a container of brightly colored compostable containers. Arlo gives me one of his trademark wide grins. We don't call him Prince Charming for nothing.

I sigh heavily. I'd rather be at our headquarters drinking craft beer and listening to Van Halen, but it's too early to bail out of Arlo's party. Besides, as the President of the MC I need to make sure my guys have a good time and no one gives us any trouble.

"Set up a tab on this." I pull my credit card from my wallet. "Put anything my boys ask for on there."

The bartender looks at the card uncertainly. His eyes flick upwards to the left hand corner of the bar. I follow his gaze to a security camera attached to the overhang of the bar. Axel keeps his beady eye on everything that goes on at the resort and especially at White Out.

"Clear it with Axel first if you need to."

I don't want to make this young guy feel awkward for doing his job. I place a hundred dollar bill on the counter. "And look after my boys tonight."

He nods uncertainly but pockets the bill.

I look at the camera and give Axel a wave. Son of a bitch needs to get out more if he's still spending every night behind his bank of monitors.

A new song starts, and there's a whoop from the dance floor. I guess it's better than hanging out down here.

The guys join me at the bar, and Arlo hands out the shots. I knock it back, feeling the burn, and chase it with the beer I just ordered.

That's the last shot I'll have tonight. I'm too old for this shit.

Some of the younger guys head toward the dance floor, and I slide into a booth with Quentin. His huge thighs scrape the underside of the table. That's why we call him Barrels. He's the biggest guy in the MC. That, and the fact that he runs the brewery for the club.

"You not dancing, Prez?" Quentin asks.

"What the fuck do you think?"

He chuckles, and we each sip our beer. It's a prestigious brand that suits the clientele who come here, but it lacks flavor. I can tell Quentin's thinking the same thing by the way he swirls it around in his mouth. When you run a brewery and craft beer bar, you become quite the connoisseur.

Barrels finally swallows, and his face screws up in a wince. "Tastes like piss."

"It's not gonna win any awards, that's for sure."

"Too sweet, tastes like caramel." Quentin holds the bottle up to the light and swishes the brown liquid around. "And the viscosity's too dense."

My younger self would be laughing his ass off if he could see me now. Discussing the taste notes and viscosity of the beer I'm drinking. My younger self was out to get drunk, and that was it. Taste didn't even come into it.

Thank fuck I grew up.

Travis joins us, and him and Quentin start discussing their entry for the state craft beer awards. An award would be great for business and it's an achievement for the guys, validation that they're doing something right.

Validation's important when you're running a team. I want to make my boys feel like they're achieving something.

They're all ex-military, and half of them broken. Not all the boys came out tonight; Lone Star can't stand to be around most people, Spec's PTSD can be triggered by loud noises, and Davis still has a hang up about his hearing aids.

I'm thinking about Davis, the young prospect, as I slowly sip my beer. I should have pushed him more, insisted he come out. It would have done him good to be around a young crowd.

He gave some lame excuse about not wanting to leave his new puppy alone, but we all knew it's because of his loss of hearing. It would have done him good to talk to a pretty girl tonight, give him some confidence. My men are hooking up like we're running a dating agency. There must be a woman for him somewhere.

I'm lost in my thoughts, but I notice the change in the air when she walks in. My head jerks up towards the door, and my breath catches in my chest.

The woman pauses on the threshold of the club, and her thick dark hair, artfully curled, bounces over her exposed shoulders. She's tall like her father and made more so by the six inch heels she's wearing that make her legs look longer. Her red dress ends above the knee, and there's a hint of thick thighs and delicious promises.

My hungry gaze scans her body, taking in every curve. The way the dress cinches in at the waist and the tight bodice pushes her oversized breasts against the fabric, forcing a pillowing cleavage that makes my throat dry.

Her face has a thick coat of makeup covering her already flawless skin. But it's her eyes that have me spellbound. Emerald green. They scan the room taking everything in, intelligent and with a wariness much older than her years.

The music slows as she walks in. That's what it feels like, but maybe it's just me as my heartbeat speeds up and my pulse quickens. Blood thunders through my ears so loudly I can't hear anything.

The air shifts. It parts for her as she struts into the club. Strut is the only word for how she walks. Her delicate beaded purse hangs off her bent elbow, and the two friends she's with totter on their heels to catch up.

Quentin turns to see what I'm staring at, and his mouth drops open.

"Is that…?"

"Isabella Berone." Her name rumbles out of my chest like a growl. The mafia princess whose father has a deadly reputation.

I haven't seen her since she was an adolescent playing at the lake. Her father keeps her tightly guarded, and I can see why.

My dick's hard as stone, and my heart's pounding. I glance around the club, and every other hot blooded man is staring at her. My fists clench under the table, and I'm overcome with an urge to break the heads of every single one of them.

What the hell she's doing out without a security

detail I have no idea, but not a single man in here is going to get near her tonight.

"Get the guys," I growl without taking my eyes off Isabella.

She shouldn't be here. She can't be more than eighteen. I'm damn sure her father doesn't know where she is, and it won't go well for any hot headed man who tries to touch her.

But it's not because of her father that I call my guys together. Isabella may only be eighteen, but I'll make damn sure no one gets near her. No one but me.

2
ISABELLA

The club is packed, and people are staring at me. So much for going incognito. It's my first time in a night club, and I thought everyone would be more dressed up. I can see why my little red dress and killer heels might be a bit much.

I chose White Out at The Emerald Heart Resort because it's full of tourists, so hopefully no one knows who I am and can report back to my father.

Still, I wish I'd worn something a bit more inconspicuous, even if I do look cute in this red dress.

But it's too late now.

I do what my aunt taught me to do when you're feeling unsure. I square my shoulders, stick my chin out, and flounce to the bar as if I own the place.

The bartender has his finger pressed to his headset when I arrive at the bar, which is good because it gives me time to figure out what the hell to order.

Cassie and Jude come up behind me. Cassie tugs on her tight skirt, trying to pull it down.

"I feel like a slut in this," she mutters.

"But you look gorgeous." I flash her a confident smile, hoping some of it will rub off on my friend.

She glances around nervously. Neither of them were too keen when I put forward the idea of sneaking out and coming to the club.

Dad thinks I'm at a sleepover at Cassie's. She's lucky her parents don't give a shit what she does. The irony is that all she wants to do is stay home and read, whereas my father keeps me practically locked in the house and all I want to do is go out and have some fun, dance to music, and talk to a cute boy.

I was the one who organized the fake IDs and came up with the plan to evade my security detail. I crushed up sleeping pills and put them in the hot chocolate I so thoughtfully bought out to their car while dressed in my pajamas an hour ago. When we sneaked past them to get the Uber, they were fast asleep with their mouths open.

The bartender gives a curt nod and takes his hand off his headset, then turns his attention to us. "Ladies, we'd like to offer you the VIP area this evening."

He smiles warmly, and I give Cassie a nudge. "See, that's what happens when you dress up."

"Follow my colleague please, and he'll take you right up there with a round of vodka cocktails on the house."

I glance behind us where a man in a dark suit is standing. He's got a headset on too and looks like he's with the club's security. My heart sinks, thinking we've been found out already. But he smiles warmly, putting me at ease.

"This way, ladies."

I'm used to this kind of special treatment but Cassie and Jude follow me nervously, twittering behind their hands.

I take my time in my heels, enjoying the attention we're getting as we walk past the dance floor. I purposely turn my head away. I'll scan the floor from upstairs and see if there are any cute guys to dance with. That is if any of them are brave enough to approach me.

As I walk through the club, we pass a line of booths and a group of older men sitting at one drinking beer.

My gaze is drawn to the man on the end. He's older than the others, his dark hair flecked with silver and the lines of a good life etched on his face. He's sitting casually, his legs splayed under the booth and one hand on his beer, oozing confidence and clearly the leader of these men.

He's got a rough beard and wears leather pants and a button-down shirt where a tattoo snakes up one side of his neck. So different from the clean cut men I'm used to being around. No Italian suit and manicures for this man.

As I walk past, we lock eyes and he holds my gaze. Most men are intimidated by who I am, who my father is, and I'm not used to a stranger openly staring at me. Especially in the way he's staring, like he wants to devour me.

He takes a sip of beer, not breaking eye contact, and I notice his big hands. I bet there are calluses on the palms and dirt under his fingernails. I bet he knows what to do with his big hands.

My breath catches, and heat spreads up my neck. I've never blushed in my life and I break the eye contact, horrified that a man can make my body react in this way.

Even as I turn from him, I feel his gaze still on me. Maybe it's not a cute boy I'll dance with tonight but a scorching hot man.

I'm following the doorman up the stairs, but I risk a glance back at the stranger. He's still staring at me. I give him a smile, and he frowns and looks away.

The rejection takes my breath away. I've never been rejected in my life. Fury courses through my veins. I gave him an opening, and he spurned me.

Who the fuck does he think he is? Then I remember that no one here knows me. He doesn't know I'm Isabella Berone, only daughter of the infamous Carlo Berone. A member of the only mafia family on Wild Heart Mountain.

The bartender unclips a black cord threaded with gold, and we enter the VIP area. The seats here are plush velvet, and we're looking down on the entire club. But I'm disappointed. I wanted to dance tonight. I wanted to flirt and have fun with real people.

A moment later, a tray of drinks turns up.

"I'm Gregg," says the waiter, placing three cocktails on the table. "I'll be your personal waiter tonight. If you need anything, push the button right here."

He indicates a button on the edge of the booth. As soon as he's gone, Jude leans in and grabs a cocktail. She sniffs it suspiciously.

"Why are they giving us the special treatment?" She frowns at the cocktail but takes a sip.

I shrug my shoulders. "Why wouldn't they?"

"Because it's not normal, that's why. People usually pay good money for VIP areas."

I raise my eyebrows at her, because as far as I know she's never been to a club before either.

"I mean, I guess they do," she mumbles as she takes another sip.

"Don't worry. Just enjoy yourself."

I stand up and head to the railing to look out over the club. Jude's words have me rattled. Why are they giving us special treatment? They can't know who I am, can they?

My gaze scans the club, but it's not cute boys on the dance floor that I'm looking for. My gaze darts all over the place until I spot him. The handsome stranger. He's moved from his booth, and he's leaning over a railing near the dance floor right at the bottom of the stairs that leads up here. He's also looking straight up at me.

My breath catches in my throat, and my mouth goes dry. He is definitely the best looking man I've ever seen. Even for an older man.

I break the eye contact, but my pulse still races.

If someone has recognized me, then it won't be long until my father turns up to drag me home. I came out to have some fun, and that's exactly what I'm going to do.

Feeling suddenly thirsty, I grab my cocktail and slurp half of it down. It doesn't taste like I expected vodka to taste. It just tastes like cranberry and grapefruit juice. But the only other alcohol I've ever had is the occasional red wine at dinner and amaretto at Christmas, so what do I know?

"I'm going to the bathroom," I tell my friends. "Why don't you guys go dance?"

Cassie shakes her head. "I'm good here. I like observing."

Jude nods in agreement. "Me too."

They cling to their drinks, and I have to smile at my friends. I dragged them out here, and I love that they both went along with my scheme despite clearly not wanting to be here.

I give them both a spontaneous hug.

"What's that for?" says Cassie laughing.

I shrug. "Just to let you know I love you guys."

Then I turn and head down the stairs.

3
RAIDEN

My body vibrates from the close proximity of the speaker, and my ears will be ringing for hours. But my position by the dance floor was the best place to keep an eye on Isabella.

When I explained the situation to my men, they each took up positions around the club. If any scumbag tries anything with Isabella, one of my guys will be on hand to step in.

I suspect Axel knows she's here by the way she was taken up to the VIP booth. Why the hell he's letting Isabella Berone drink in his club, I have no idea. I'll have to ask him all about it at the next poker night. But she's here now, and at least we'll be able to tell her father we did our best to protect her.

But it's not for the sake of Isabella's father that I'm positioned where I can watch her. I'm racked with jealousy, and the thought of another man talking to Isabella has my fists clenching by my sides.

I watch their cocktails being delivered. These girls are too young to drink, and I hope Axel knows what he's doing. It's a dangerous game to get on the wrong side of Carlo Berone.

Isabella saunters over to the railing and comes into view. My chest tightens; she's fucking gorgeous. Full of confidence as she surveys the room. Like a fucking queen looking down on her subjects.

Her gaze meets mine, and for the second time our eyes lock. She stares at me, and I wonder what she's thinking. Earlier she smiled at me, a small coy smile. A smile any man would cherish coming from a woman like her. A flirty smile that set my pulse racing.

She's got no business smiling at men like that. It'll get her into trouble if she smiles at every man she looks at like that.

I'm not about to let that happen. I've had my eyes on the VIP booth ever since.

There's no smile this time, and she breaks the eye contact first. She steps back from the railing and disappears from view.

It feels like the room got colder.

But a few moments later, there's movement on the stairs. A slim heel comes into view followed by a pair of luscious legs. She's gripping the rail to steady herself. It can't be easy descending stairs in those heels, but she still manages to look graceful.

My heart's battering against my chest, and my dick grinds against my zipper as it hardens.

I drink her in. All eighteen years of her. Christ, she's the same age as my daughter.

The thought has me running a hand through my hair as she saunters over to me.

I'm here to protect her, that's all. I won't do anything stupid like throw her over my shoulder and take her back to the club like I'm longing to do.

"Hey," she says, tilting her head.

Most women her age would be shy talking to an older man, but she comes straight up to me, bold as anything.

"Hi."

My gaze takes in her face now that we're closer. Her plump lips are tinged with red lipstick, and her emerald green eyes are illuminated by colorful makeup. It's pretty, but I long to run my thumb over it. To smudge it away and see how she looks without the paint.

"I'm Trina."

She holds out a hand, and I resist the urge to raise my eyebrows. I shouldn't be surprised she's going under a false name tonight. She must have used a fake ID to get into the club.

"Hi Trina." Her hand is cool in mine, her fingers soft. I clasp it too long, not wanting to let go. "I'm Raiden."

We stare at each other, our gazes locked and our hands entwined. Electricity sparks between us, and heat spreads up my arm and courses through my body. I want to pull her close, to claim her plump lips. To take her away from here and equal parts tell her off for coming to a place like this and kiss her senseless.

Then I remember her age. Fuck. She's eighteen, barely legal. I've got no right to fantasize over a woman who's barely out of girlhood.

I drop her hand, and disappointment flashes across her face before she resets it in a well-used mask.

"What's the occasion?" she asks.

I cock my head, wondering what she means. She turns to look around the club.

"You're out with a bunch of men. Two over there." She indicates the edge of the dance floor.

"Two over there." She indicates the booths. "And two hanging out by the restrooms." She indicates Barrels and Travis, who I positioned by the bathrooms to make sure the ladies weren't harassed if they needed the restroom.

"Someone should tell those two it's not the best place to meet women. They come across as creepy."

I smile despite myself. She's observant, smart, *and* funny.

"How do you know they're with me?"

She tilts her head and half smiles. "Come on. You're the only ones in here with beards and tattoos, and you're about twice the age of the other clientele."

I mock wince.

"I didn't mean to offend you," she says with a smile so sweet I almost beg her to insult me again.

"We're at a bachelor party. My friend over there's getting married."

I indicate Arlo who's dancing with Colter, making sure the dance floor is safe if the ladies decide to venture out there.

She bites her lower lip, thinking. "Then why are you all spread out around the club? Don't you like each other?"

Damn, she's too smart for her own good. But I can't tell her it's for her protection. That even though

I only laid eyes on her a matter of minutes ago, she's the same age as my daughter, and she's the only daughter of a dangerous man, the feeling of protectiveness I have over her is so strong my chest hurts.

Instead, I change the subject.

"How about you? What occasion brought you out tonight?"

She eyes me, obviously not happy that I didn't answer her question, but she doesn't press.

"Girls just want to have fun, don't you know? We don't need an occasion to come out."

You do when you're Carlo Berone's daughter. But I let her have her moment of fun. I'm sure she doesn't get to do this much.

"And are you?" She cocks her head, unsure what I'm referring to. "Having fun?"

She leans in to hear me above the music, and I catch the sweet scent of gardenias. I can't tell if it's from her hair or her perfume, and I resist the urge to pull her to me and find out.

"I am now."

She smiles at me from under thickly coated eyelashes, and even as my heart swells at the attention, another part of me wants to march her out of here and tell her off for flirting with a man like me.

"How old are you, Trina?"

The smile slides off her face. She's angry I'm not flirting along. But I'm too old to play games.

"Twenty-one."

She holds my gaze as she says it, never once showing any indication of the lie. Damn, she's good.

I raise my eyebrows, but she keeps her gaze steady.

"That's a coincidence. I'm twenty-one too."

She laughs at my obvious lie, and it's a genuine laugh that makes her eyes sparkle like sunshine on a mountain lake.

There's movement by the door, and we both turn to see three men in tailored suits enter the club.

"Puttana…" Isabella rattles off a stream of Italian curses. Fear flashes across her face and she glances around wildly, looking for an escape.

For one crazy moment I think about dragging her to the fire exit and making off with her on the back of my bike. What would happen if I kidnapped the eighteen year old daughter of Carlo Berone? It wouldn't just be me he'd come after. He'd destroy the entire MC. I can't do that to my men.

Besides, it's one thing to flirt with an older man. There's no way a woman like Isabella could be attracted to a man like me: twice her age, rough, and bearded. She's used to the clean shaven well-dressed men who work for her father, to being driven around in the back on a tinted SUV, not on the back of a Harley.

Still, when I see the desperation in her expression, I know I'd risk everything for her. I clasp her hand.

"Isabella." She looks up at me in surprise, her eyes wide because I know who she is. The confusion turns to anger.

"Did you call him?"

"No." I shake my head. "But you must have known you would be recognized."

She frowns even as she nods her head.

"I thought we'd have more time," she mutters to herself, and I don't know if she means she'd have more time at the club or more time with me.

I glance up at the men, and they've spotted her. They're moving toward us, and at the same time my men are heading this way too, ready to back me up if needed.

"Why don't you want to go back?" I ask urgently. "Does he hurt you?"

I've heard about Carlo's cruelty, but she's got enough flesh on display and I haven't seen any evidence of harm.

"No." She shakes her head. "My dad would never hurt a woman."

Relief floods me. I'd risk everything if she was in any danger.

"He's strict. I can't go anywhere. I can't have any fun." She slumps against the barrier to the dance floor, defeated.

So it's fun she's so desperate for, not to escape harm. She might not like the way her father keeps her guarded, but she's not in danger.

The men approach and stop before us. My men form a circle behind. The dance floor has stopped moving and the entire club is staring, apart from a drunk group in the corner who keep on singing loudly and out of tune.

I don't want to cause trouble for Axel, but damned if I'll let her go if she doesn't want to.

"Come with us, please."

One of the men holds an arm out for Isabella.

She looks at me, and there's a sadness in her eyes. "It was nice to meet you, Raiden. Or should I call you Prez?"

It's my turn to be surprised. She knew who I was all along. She gives me a small smile, and for a moment the flirtatiousness is back.

Then she stands up straight, squares her shoulders, and looks the man dead in the eye.

"Let's go," she commands as if she's running the show and not being dragged away by her father.

Her friends have come down from the VIP area, and they trail behind hanging their heads and looking like they're about to burst into tears. There'll be a few sets of angry parents tonight when they find out where their daughters have been.

My men look to me, and I shake my head. I won't cause a scene, and I won't risk them because a pretty girl wants to have some fun. But it still doesn't sit easy with me.

There's a bar next to the dance floor, and I scribble my number on a coaster.

I catch up with Isabella as she's shrugging into her coat in the foyer.

Axel has come down from whatever tower he was hiding in and he speaks to the men quietly, no doubt pleading his case to Carlo.

While the men are distracted, I slip Isabella the coaster. It's got a picture of a palm tree and a cold beer on it even though this club is in the mountains.

"You ever need any help, anything at all, you call me."

She nods once, and our eyes lock. A spark jumps between us that's so strong I think my heart might combust.

"Thank you," she whispers and pockets the coaster just as the men turn around.

I back away quickly, not wanting to get her in

any more trouble. Isabella straightens up and doesn't even give me a backward glance as she struts off, her friends tottering behind her and the men jogging to catch up with her long confident strides.

I stand motionless for a long time after they've left, breathing in the scent of gardenias that lingers in the air.

4
ISABELLA

Two Years Later…

Low moans come from behind the mahogany doors. I glance at the man standing to attention beside the door.

"How long has he been like this?"

The man keeps his gaze straight ahead. "Since before lunch."

"Figlio de puttana …"

The man doesn't even flinch at my cuss words. It's one of my favorite things, swearing in Italian. Papa's always trying to get me to speak it more, and it's one of my little rebellions against him. I only ever speak Italian when I'm swearing.

But today is not the day to be at war with my father.

I turn the handle and step into the room. Despite the sunny day, it's dark and cool inside. The only light comes from a sliver of sunlight pushing between a crack in the thick curtains.

My eyes take a moment to adjust before I make out my father.

He's slumped in the armchair by the empty grate of the fireplace. An empty bottle of red wine is upturned on the coffee table with a stained wine glass beside it.

I slip into the room and close the door behind me. Papa doesn't even look up, which frightens me. He's usually vigilant, on guard at all times, but not today.

There's a photo album spread out on the coffee table. It's open to the page of my christening. My mother holds me up to the camera while the priest sprinkles holy water on my head. My chubby baby face is contorted into an intense frown, and my father always brings this moment up, saying that even as a baby I had a mistrust of authority.

The other photos are of my parents, much younger and happier. My father's face is unlined and wearing a smile that I seldom see these days.

I close the photo album and crouch next to my

father. He has his head in his hands, his fingers splayed as he weeps into them.

"Papa?"

I put my hand gently on his shoulder, but he doesn't stir.

It's alarming seeing the mighty Carlo Berone like this, and if any of his enemies saw him, they'd know his weakness. But it's only one day of the year. One day that he allows himself to grieve.

"Papa," I say again, gently prying his hands from his face. My hair falls onto his arm, and it finally alerts him to my presence.

He lifts his red eyes to mine, and the tear-stained face is so out of character for the father I know that I almost recoil. But I've seen him like this before.

Once every year on the anniversary of my mother's death. It's an indulgence he allows himself. Because every other time he has to bury his grief, hide it deep inside himself to protect his reputation.

"Piccina." He calls me by my childhood nickname even though I'm a woman of twenty. I let him have that indulgence once a year too.

His hand lands on my head and a watery smile appears on his features as he strokes my hair.

"You look so much like her, Piccina. So beautiful."

I've heard this before. Apparently I inherited my

mother's beauty and my father's temper. A lethal combination.

I have none of my mother's good grace that makes the anniversary of her death into a day of grieving for the entire estate. Many of the men and women working here still remember my mother. Some of my father's younger foot soldiers remember her from their childhoods. She loved children and had an open door policy. Any kid on the estate could come into her home and she'd feed them, play with them, laugh with them.

When she took me to the lake to swim or the park to play, she'd gather up whichever children were around and we'd all go.

Everyone loved my mother, but no one more so than my father.

"Have you had anything to eat?"

It's late afternoon, but if Papa's been drinking since breakfast, he'll need a good meal and time to sleep it off.

"So beautiful…" He shakes his head sadly, completely ignoring my question. "That's why I have to do what I'm doing, Isabella. It's for your own good."

I resist the urge to pull away. Today is hard enough on my father. I wanted to get through it without an argument.

"How can it be for my own good when it's not what I want?"

He shakes his head sadly. "You don't understand, Piccina. It is the old ways; you are too American."

I snort, because our family have lived in this country for at least three generations. We're all American, it's just my father who clings onto some out of date Italian ideal. But I bite my tongue. Not today. I won't argue with him today. In a few hours, if all goes according to plan, it will all work out anyway.

"I'll get you something to eat and ask someone to make the bed up in here."

I go to stand up, and he clutches my wrist. "Send Niccolo. Only Niccolo."

I nod in understanding. My father doesn't want his men seeing him like this. Niccolo is his most trusted lieutenant.

I set the empty wine bottle upright as I stand up.

My father reaches for the photo album and flicks it back open. "She was so beautiful."

He shakes his head sadly, and I wonder if he'll ever forgive himself for my mother's death. It wasn't his fault, but he doesn't see it that way. It's also why I have a security detail that follows me everywhere.

"Goodbye Papa."

I kiss his forehead and am overcome with a wave

of affection for the man who practically keeps me locked up, who has a security detail follow me everywhere, who insisted I study at home rather than risk being out on campus. But he's still my father, and I don't know if he'll ever speak to me again after what I'm about to do.

I leave him to his memories and slip out the door.

The guard stands up taller when he sees me.

"Don't let anyone in here apart from Niccolo."

"Yes, signorina."

I stride down the corridor, my heels clacking on the marble floor. Security headquarters is at the end of the corridor, and when I stride in the men stand up.

I pull my shoulders up tall. My father has taught me how to command men. He might be the boss, but they respect me.

"Niccolo." My eyes find the middle-aged man, with dark hair like my father's but less silver in it. He eyes me expectantly as if he's been waiting to be summoned. "I need a word."

We go into the private room next door, and I explain the situation. "My father needs food, something with a lot of carbs, and plenty of water. And make up the bed in the study. You'll have to do it yourself. No one sees him like this, you understand?"

"Of course." He looks wounded as if I'm questioning his loyalty. "It's the same every year, Isabella."

It is, but he also knows how important it is that we keep up the façade, that no one sees how deep his grief cuts.

"Don't worry, Isabella. I'll look after your father."

I nod quickly, suddenly overwhelmed by the tears that sting my eyes. I resist the urge to give Niccolo a hug because I haven't given him a hug since I was a little girl, and he's too smart. He'd get suspicious.

"Thank you."

I march out of there as if I own the place, which I kind of do. My father never remarried, and he keeps telling me how all this will be mine one day. I'm just not sure I want it.

At the end of the corridor, my personal guards Chiara and Alessia fall into step behind me. I'm so used to their constant presence that I hardly notice.

Since my escape two years ago, I have two guards shadowing me everywhere I go. And they've been instructed never to accept food or drink from me.

I've been a good little princess for the past few months, lulling them into a false sense of security.

I feel bad that they'll get in trouble for what I'm about to do. But they won't be harmed. I asked for female guards to make me feel more comfortable, and my father complied. He won't harm a woman, I tell myself as I head toward the back door.

I stop at the door to change my shoes, as I always do going into the garden, or at least as I have for the past five months. Ever since my father told me about his harebrained scheme and I knew I had to get out.

I slip my heels off and put my sneakers on. My guards think it's so the heels don't sink into the grass. They don't realize it's so I can run faster.

I saunter through the renaissance garden, resisting the urge to wipe my sweaty palms on my silk trousers. I stop at the flower garden to pick a bunch of gardenias. They were my mother's favorite.

The small, whitewashed chapel is at the edge of the property. Thick woodlands surround it on three sides where the brambles have gotten overgrown and thick. My mother rests in the chapel, and it's the one area of the estate where my father never ventures.

What only myself and Niccolo know is that it's also a blind spot. My father wanted no CCTV on the place where his late wife rests. Another old-fashioned superstition that would be worth something to his enemies if it ever got out.

They'll all know soon enough, and I'm sorry for that. But there's nothing else I can do if I want my freedom.

WILD HEART

I pause at the door of the chapel and take a deep breath. The emotion I feel is real, and I have to work to keep my shoulders from shuddering. I was six when my mother passed. Old enough to remember her and grieve what I've missed all these years.

Our bond was close, made more so because there were complications with the birth and she wasn't able to conceive again after I was born. My father's older relatives told him to put her aside, that a wife who couldn't bear sons was no wife at all. It's the one thing from the old-fashioned ways that my father refused to do. He loved her too much, sons or not.

I take a deep breath and step forward. Chiara and Alessia step with me, and I pause and turn around. This is the moment I've been practicing in front of my mirror. The moment that my entire plan depends on.

I take a shuddering breath and let a single tear escape my eye. I silently offer a prayer to my mother to forgive me for using her memory to orchestrate my escape. I hope she'd understand.

"I want a few moments alone with my mother."

I don't plead. I would never do that, but I allow the grief to wash over me. For them to see the emotion on my face.

The guards look to each other, uncertain. Chiara is the most senior, and she gives me a hard look. No doubt trying to read any lie beneath my words. I'm a good liar, and she doesn't detect any.

I also know she lost her mother when she was twelve. It's why I asked if she could be my head guard.

"Of course, signorina." She nods her head and takes a step back. "We'll be right outside. You have your privacy."

I bow my head in thanks so she doesn't see the relief that floods me. The hardest part of my plan was getting past the guards. And I've done it without raising suspicion.

I will myself to slow down as I cross the threshold and enter the cool chapel.

My mother's grave is to the left of the apse in pride of place. I walk slowly in case the guards change their mind and decide to come in after me.

When I reach her shrine, I lay the flowers and say a quick prayer.

"I'm sorry, Mamma. I hope you understand that I can't live like this."

I cross myself and say the Hail Mary.

My hand goes to my pocket, and I pull out the well-worn coaster that the Prez of a motorcycle club gave me two years ago. My thumb runs over the number, almost faded now but committed to memory.

There's been many times over the past two years that I longed to call Raiden just to hear his voice. He's the first person I thought of when my father told me my fate.

But why drag him into it? It would only end badly for him. If he helped me escape, my father would show him no mercy.

Besides, while I thought we were flirting in the club that night two years ago, it's obvious he knew who I was all along. He was only speaking to me to keep me there. Whether he knew my father's men were coming or whether he wanted to keep me safe, probably to earn favor with my father, he had his reasons, and it wasn't because he was interested in me.

I've since learned he has a daughter the same age as me. He was behaving like a protective father. That's why he gave me his number to use if I ever really needed help. If I texted him for a chat, he'd think I was nuts.

I pocket the coaster quickly. I'll never use the number, but I like having it with me. I can't explain why, but it makes me feel safe, like maybe if everything went bad, I'd still have an eject button.

A glance at the door tells me the guards are still outside in the afternoon sun. Moving quickly, I retrieve the backpack that I stashed under the front pew two days ago.

On silent feet, I move to the back room of the chapel and the window where I've been unscrewing the latch one turn at a time. The room is full of dried flowers, a hobby I took up a few months back. Usually Chiara is in here with me, and I work on the window, one turn of the screw at a time, when her back is turned.

Today, I turn the screw a few times and the latch clicks open. I wince at the noise the window makes, the hinges creaky with rust.

It's hard to hear over the hammering of my heart, but I don't hear any footsteps. If one of the guards came in now, I could explain this away. I could say I needed fresh air, that I left the bag the last time I was here, which is true.

It's my final chance to stay. I don't take it.

I throw my bag through the window and climb out.

The branches are thick, but by swinging my weight I make it to the back wall of the estate.

Cassie happened to take up indoor rock climbing a few months ago, and I begged my father to let me do it with her. She thought the idea was her own and not one I'd planted in her mind with suggestive techniques. I feel bad manipulating my friend that way, and I hope she doesn't get in trouble for it. I'm sure she'll understand when she finds out my reasons.

The wall is worn back here where old brambles have pressed into it over decades. I launch my bag over the wall, and there are enough holds to scramble up. Then I'm over the wall and dropping down the other side to freedom.

5
RAIDEN

"This the place?" Marcus squints at the flashing neon sign that promises 'Girls Girls Girls.' He looks as dubious as I feel, and I check the address on my phone.

"Yup."

The Fuzzy Peach strip club is tucked down a winding alleyway off the inner city streets of Charlotte.

It's late afternoon, not yet dusk, as a group of men weave drunkenly past us. One stops to take a piss in a doorway that leads to a vape store.

"If that piss trickles down to my bike…" Marcus shakes his head slowly, not needing to finish his sentence. I know exactly what he'll do if piss gets on his bike, and it won't be pretty.

"Stay here with the bikes."

I'm not leaving my baby in a place like this. Not where there are drunk men with obviously no respect for themselves or personal property.

"Why don't I get to see the titties, Prez?"

His grin makes it obvious he's joking. We both know if he wanted to go to a titty bar, it wouldn't be a rough joint like this. There are much classier establishments if you know where to find them.

"Trust me, I wish we were meeting somewhere else. Anywhere else but here," I mutter as I watch the doorman shove a customer onto the street. The man stumbles and falls, cursing loudly. The doorman stays staunch, and the man gets to his feet and drifts off.

"Any trouble just holler," I say to Marcus.

"You got it, Prez."

He relaxes against his bike, the causal stance hiding the alertness that he's trained for. Marcus was an Army Ranger. His specialty was reconnaissance. He's six foot three and as solid as the logs his family mills. His road name is Wood, and not just because of the fact that his family have run the Wild Sawmill for generations. He's also good with his hands, crafting little animal sculptures and ornaments out of any bit of wood he finds.

As I leave, his hands go to his pocket and he pulls out a hunk of wood and a small knife. The wing of an owl is half carved as he chips away at the piece, his knife making a skimming sound with every stroke.

I smile to myself as I walk away. There's nothing as casually menacing as an ex-military mountain man slowly carving a chunk of wood while leaning against a badass Harley and wearing an MC patch.

The doorman eyes me up and down as I approach, then steps aside to let me pass. It's a sign of how rough this establishment is that they let me in with my cut on.

Through the door is a short corridor, and a plastic curtain leads to the main bar. Music thumps through the floor, and it stinks like sweat and desperation.

Girls twirl on the stage looking bored as rowdy customers wave dollar bills at them. One of the girls on the stage steps away from her pole and bends down slowly to collect the money, letting one lucky customer slide it into the waist of her thong.

She looks bored and tired, and I wonder if she needs the money to feed her kids. I'd like to buy her a decent meal and find her a better job.

But it's not the women I'm here to save.

I walk around the end of the stage and to the far side of the room, scanning the faces of the men I pass.

He's not with the groups gathered at the side of the stage or sitting at the tables nearest the stage, which is what I expected. On the other side of the room are booths where the light doesn't quite reach.

It's the glint of metal that I see first, a wheelchair tucked under the end of a table. The man in the chair is slumped with his hand resting on his elbows watching the girls dance. There're three empty beer bottles sitting on the table, and he watches the stage with glassy eyes.

"Jesus."

The kid's as bad as his parents told me he was. I approach the table and slide into the chair opposite him.

"Strangest place I've ever conducted a job interview."

The kid lifts his dark eyes to me while never moving.

"I don't want the job."

His eyes move lazily back to the stage. They're expressionless as he watches a girl swing her legs around a pole and hang upside down.

I scratch the side of my beard, taking my time. If he's trying to shock me, it's not going to work.

"I was in Iraq with your old man."

The kid doesn't even blink.

"If you're about to give me some spiel about getting my life back, you're wasting your breath."

He keeps his gaze on the woman and his expression neutral.

He's given up. I've seen it before, and it only make me more determined to help him.

"I told my dad I didn't want to see you." He looks back at me. "No offense. But I don't need some motorcycle gang. I'm in a fucking wheelchair. I can't ride."

He spits the last bit out, and his bitterness is a relief. It means he's angry, but he also still feels something, so there's still hope.

I nod slowly and lean back in the chair, watching the dancers for a while. A minute goes by and then another. The boy keeps his eyes on the dancing, but I can tell he's curious as to why I'm still here.

I observe him out of the corner of my eye. He's twenty-five, but with his sunken eyes and hangdog expression he looks older.

His father told me he used to be fit. He loved to run and ride and race bikes. He's loved everything about bikes since he was a kid. He went into the army as a motorcycle mechanic until his convoy got hit moving between bases.

He came back home minus both his legs. A double amputee from above the knee.

That was twenty months ago. But despite the therapy and rehab, he spends his nights drinking and frequenting places like this.

His father called me in desperation to see if there was anything we could do.

"I heard you worked in Mechanic Maintenance."

The boy blinks lazily. "Yeah."

"What you know about Harleys?"

He shrugs. "I know I'll never get on one again."

I rub my beard, trying not to feel sorry for the kid. He doesn't need my pity. There're all sorts of adaptations these days. The kid could ride, but it takes more than an adapted bike. He's got to want to do it.

"I don't need you to get on one. I need you to get under one."

His gaze flicks to mine, and for the first time there's interest.

"I'm looking for a mechanic. Someone who knows bikes. And I hear you're the man for the job."

"I already told my old man I'm not interested. I'm sorry, Mr.... you've wasted your time."

I move the beer bottles away to the other end of the table and lean forward. "I don't think you're a waste of time. In fact, Luke, I think you're just the man we need."

"I'm not a charity case," he hisses.

I sit back away from his intense gaze. Damn, the kid's got it bad.

"And I'm not a charity."

"You are." He sits up for the first time and turns his head away from the stage. "My old man told me about you, taking in broken veterans who need help. Well, I don't need your help."

He puts his hands on his wheelchair and reverses out from under the table. I stand up and move over to him, pulling a card out of my back pocket.

"I'm sorry you feel that way. We're ex-military men who love to ride. We're not a charity, and I expect anyone who works for me to work hard and follow my rules. I don't dish out pity, and I'm not your therapist. But I can offer you a job and a place to stay so you can conduct your life with dignity and self-respect."

He stares at the card in my hand for a long time.

"What do you ride?" he asks finally.

"A Fat Boy 114. It's parked out front if you want to take a look. As long as someone hasn't pissed on it."

A ghost of a smile passes across his face, and he reluctantly takes the card from my hand.

"At least let my man show you where the classy strip joints are."

"I'll think about it."

It's the most I'm going to get out of him. I sure as hell hope the kid snaps out of his own sorrow. It's hard to readjust to civilian life, especially with life-changing injuries like his.

"Come for a visit, take a look around, meet the guys, see the shop and see if you like it."

"Maybe," he grunts and wheels over to the bar. I let him go, knowing I won't get an answer today. I only hope I've done enough to convince him to at least visit.

The music changes, and someone announces a brand new dancer. The room whoops, and the lights dim.

"Shit."

I don't want to be here for this. There's a throng of men pushing toward the stage, and it takes me a while before I can move past them.

I'm passing the stage just as the curtain opens and a long thick leg in killer heels peeks out from behind the curtain.

My skin prickles with heat, and blood rushes to my dick. Shit, after all these years I'm just as horny as the men in here, getting excited about a piece of flesh.

I should keep moving through the crowd but I'm rooted in place, needing to see the owner of that leg. The curtain parts and the little minx is stepping backwards, shuffling her chunky ass through the curtain, shaking it so the tiny skirt she's wearing shimmers under the disco lights.

Long dark hair flows over her shoulders and down her back. She's got a tiny golden top on to match her skirt and most of her back is exposed, showing enticing curvy flesh.

"You see something you like?"

I didn't notice Luke wheel up next to me. He's wearing the first grin I've seen him in all night. I'm aware that it's because my jaw is on the floor and my black jeans are suddenly too tight around my hard cock.

I don't usually have this reaction to a woman. Not since that night two years ago when I was in the White Out and ran into Isabella Berone…

A strangled noise burbles out of my throat as realization hits. At the same time, the woman turns around with a flick of her neck. Silky thick hair whips around her shoulders, and the men whoop as her beautiful features are revealed.

"What the fuck…?"

6
ISABELLA

My stomach pulls into a tight knot at the sound of the men baying to see my flesh.

I've never had to paint my mask on so thickly as I'm doing right now. I give a brilliant smile as if there's nowhere I'd rather be than shaking my booty on stage in front of a room full of drunken men.

The catcalls make my stomach churn and I fight the bile in my throat, swallowing it down as I turn to face my audience.

Bright lights flash onto the stage, making me blink. I can only make out the shapes of men as they crowd around the edges of the stage waving dollar bills at me.

It's the best performance of my life as I strut

down the stage as if it's a fashion runway and not sticky with beer and God knows what else.

I'm the classiest woman they'll see on stage tonight, and they know it. I'm not saying that to be mean. The women I've met backstage are courageous in a way I'll never be. They've been kind and sympathetic to my first night nerves, more than one offering me a smoke or a pill to calm them. The only thing I took was a shot of cheap vodka that burned my throat on the way down and did nothing to settle my stomach.

I hate not being able to see the crowd, and my heart thunders in time to the music. What if my father was right? What if his enemies are out there and watching me?

The last twenty-four hours without a security detail have been thrilling. I've felt free but also a little lonely. I didn't realize how comforting the quiet presences of Chiara and Alessia were.

I say a quick prayer for my former guards hoping my father isn't being too hard on them.

After I scaled the fence yesterday, I jogged into the woods and took a path that winds around the mountain and comes out near the town of Hope and the train station.

With my hair tucked into a cap, I boarded the first train to Raleigh and then doubled back to Charlotte.

I wandered the streets until I found the perfect hotel. Nothing too swanky, nothing too cheap, and not too close to the train station. The proprietor didn't bat an eyelid when I paid in cash.

All I need is a few nights at The Fuzzy Peach, and it should be enough to stop my father's plans. There are plenty of classier strip joints in town, but my father or his business associates own half of them. This place was perfect, small and run down. Managed by a not too bright local who didn't recognize me when I turned up looking for work.

As I strut down the stage to the sound of catcalls and lewd remarks, I'm questioning the solidness of my plan. The men are drunker than I imagined and less respectful.

One of them waves bills at me, and I ignore him. I'm not bending over for less than a hundred.

"Show us your tits!" someone yells.

I resist the urge to kick my heel in his face and instead turn around while bending my knees into a halfway slut drop.

From the direction of the mouthy guy, there's the sound of a fist connecting to a face. A man screams, literally screams, and then some asshole's climbing onto the stage.

I stagger backwards, blinking in the lights as the familiar shape of a man saunters toward me.

"No freaking way."

Raiden, President of the Wild Riders MC and the man who's haunted my dreams for the past two years is striding toward me, and he looks pissed.

There's a commotion behind him, and a man with a bloody face lunges for the stage.

"What the fuck, man?" he yells.

Raiden cracks his knuckles, and I have time to register that he's the one who punched the loudmouth. But it doesn't explain what the heck he's doing on my stage.

The relief I feel at seeing Raiden is all confused with anger that he's ruining my escape plan.

"What are you doing here?" I hiss.

"What am I...?" His expression is thunderous as he grabs my wrist, his thick hand wrapping all the way around it. "What the fuck are you doing here, Isabella?"

He jerks me toward him, and if he wasn't so angry it would be sexy. I bump into his body and up against his hard chest.

"You don't belong here."

He turns and drags me after him, and his hold on me is so tight I have no choice but to follow. I totter on my heels to keep up with him, and that fuels my anger even more. Isabella Berone runs after no man.

I flick my hair over my shoulders and try to

maintain some dignity as I'm dragged off the stage and through the club.

"Get the fuck out of my way," Raiden growls as he elbows his way through the crowd heading toward the exit. There's a man in a wheelchair following close behind and pushing people aside who try to lunge for me.

"We'll save you, sweetheart," one of them calls.

I stick my chin up because I don't need saving, and Raiden better have a damn good reason why he's dragging me out of here.

I don't get a chance to speak to him because it's too loud, but I'll give him a piece of my mind when we get outside. Hands grab at my flesh as I pass, and instead of resisting Raiden I lean into him and pick up my pace, running as best I can in these heels.

Damn him for making me run. I'm clinging onto him and letting him shield me as we near the exit, even as waves of anger wash over me.

We pass through plastic curtains that stick to my skin and come face to face with a bouncer. His arms are folded across his chest, and he's as thick as a brick wall.

Raiden doesn't even slow his pace.

With the hand that isn't holding me, he swings a punch so quick the bouncer isn't expecting it. The man stumbles to the side, and Raiden drags me through the door and out into the cool air.

"Get the bikes ready," Raiden calls to a large man leaning against a motorbike. He's got the same Wild Riders MC jacket that Raiden's wearing, but without the President's badge.

I glance behind me, expecting to see the doorman coming after us. But instead the young guy in the wheelchair is blocking the door. He's wheeling back and forth like he doesn't know how to drive it. He moves backward and runs over the doorman's foot, eliciting a yelp of pain.

"Sorry, still not used to this thing," the man in the wheelchair says.

But he's got a grin on his face as he moves the motorized controller back and forth. The doorman bounces on his toes impatiently with a frown on his face, torn between wanting to run after us and not wanting to push a man in a wheelchair out of the way.

I kind of feel sorry for him. He's just doing his job, and I decide to throw him a bone.

"It's okay," I call to him. "I quit anyway."

All I had in the changing room was a small bag with some makeup and twenty bucks. The girls can have it.

Raiden pushes a helmet onto my head. Then he shrugs his jacket off and drapes it over my shoulders.

His buddy is already reversed and ready to go.

"Get on, Isabella," he commands.

I usually hate men telling me what to do, but he's got a set to his jaw as he glances back at the doorman.

Still, I hesitate. I'm not ready to go back to my father.

"Where will you take me?"

"Not home if that's not what you want. I'll take you to the clubhouse, and you can explain what the fuck you were doing in a strip club."

He doesn't give me time to resist. His thick hands secure me at the hips, and he lifts me up like I weigh nothing and plonks me down on his bike.

"We need to go. Now."

I nod quickly and slide my leg over the seat. It catches on something sticking out, and I feel a sharp sting. When I glance down, there's a trickle of blood oozing down my leg. I guess a tiny skirt isn't the best riding gear.

Raiden revs the engine, and I grip his waist as the bike jerks forward.

Behind us, the man in the wheelchair has gotten control of his chair, and he moves aside as the doorman lunges toward us. Men from the bar burst into the street. I recognize the owner and some of his cronies.

But they're too late. As we ride past, Raiden raises a hand to wheelchair guy. The man grins and raises his hand in response.

We burst out of the alleyway, and I grip Raiden tight as we swerve around a corner.

I'm furious at him for bursting in and ruining my plans. But I'm also so relieved to see him that my chest hurts.

As the bike settles into a steady rhythm, I lean against his solid back, letting the hum of the bike soothe me. For the first time since I scaled the wall, I feel calm.

7
RAIDEN

It's dark by the time we pull up to the clubhouse. Marcus roars in behind us, and we maneuver our bikes into the line of Harleys out back. Lately, my men have been swapping the single life for family life, and there are as many cars now as bikes, each with a baby seat in the back.

Everyone's gathering tonight for a club meal. I can only be thankful we've closed the bar and restaurant so only the club will see Isabella. Still, I want to keep her presence known to as few people as possible until I figure out what the hell is going on.

I'm equal parts furious at her for dancing in a place like that where she could have come to harm and relieved that I've got her on the back of my bike.

I saw red in the club when I realized it was

Isabella showing so much flesh to those hungry men. I would have fought every single one of them to get her out of there.

I have no idea what she's trying to pull. If it's another stunt to piss off her father, then it's a good one. A mafia princess working in a place like the Fuzzy Peach. It's not even a surprise that no one recognized her. The kind of people who frequent places like that are too ignorant to know who runs them.

Although I'm betting The Fuzzy Peach isn't one of the Berone clubs. It's not classy enough.

She's got some explaining to do, and I'm still angry when I cut the engine outside the club. There're people milling about and men hanging out around the smoker where the meat for tonight has been tenderizing all afternoon.

"Make a distraction, will you," I say to Marcus.

He nods his understanding, and I wait until he goes over there and knocks the smoker over. There are roars of outrage, and I shake my head in disbelief. Knocking over the smoker isn't what I had in mind. You don't mess with a man's meat.

But it does the trick, and all hands rush over to right the smoker and see what meat can be salvaged.

Isabella is quiet behind me, and when I slide off the bike and turn to her my breath hitches. She's straddling my bike in her tiny skirt that rides all the way up her thighs. And with my helmet framing her face and her looking up at me with wide, innocent eyes, it's all I can do not to pull her to me and kiss her painted lips.

Then I remember who she is. There's nothing innocent about Isabella Berone.

"Keep your head down," I tell her. "And don't talk to anyone."

She slides the helmet off and I take her hand firmly in mine, not risking the chance that she'll run off. Not that there's anywhere to go. The HQ is in a compound in the middle of the woods on a side of a mountain. She'd be a fool to run here, but I'm not taking any chances.

"You're hurting me," she hisses, and I loosen my grip. That's the last thing I want to do, but I don't trust her not to run.

While the men are distracted, I hustle her through the door and pull her down the corridor.

Snips and April are pressed against the wall smooching like it's the end of the world. The entire goddamn club is hooked up these days.

Snips's eyes go wide with recognition when he sees Isabella.

"Not a word to anyone."

Snips nods even though I can tell he's dying to

ask me questions. I hustle her past and pull her into the meeting room.

I lock the door behind me and pull all the blinds down. When I'm sure we're alone and no one can see, I turn to her.

She's resting with her butt against the edge of the meeting table. My jacket hangs loose on her, falling to her thighs and barely covering the poor excuse for a skirt she's wearing.

The first thing I'll need to do is find her some decent clothes.

There's blood on her leg, which makes me frown. I didn't notice she'd hurt herself. But it seems like a surface scrape.

Despite myself, my gaze travels up her body to her exposed midriff. Her Italian heritage gives her skin a tanned complexion, with dark Mediterranean hairs visible on her body. She's got a full figure, and I love that she's not afraid to show it. I long to run my hands over her skin, to feel the tiny hairs stand on end under my touch.

My cock hardens in my jeans, and I force myself to look at her face.

I desperately want to adjust my pants to ease the pain from my hard-on pressing against my zipper, but I don't want to make her any more uncomfortable than this already is.

"Start talking."

It comes out as a growl and we eye each other warily, both with our arms folded across our chests.

"What?" she says mock innocently. "Isn't a girl allowed to earn a bit of extra cash of her own?"

She's trying for a flirty tone, but the way her chest rises and falls erratically gives away the fact that she's nervous.

"You're not any girl, Isabella, and I'm sure you have enough allowance for anything you desire. Your father's not stingy."

She eyes me warily and I stare her down, trying not to get lost in her green eyes. Eventually a shiver goes through her, and she lowers her gaze.

"I wanted to shock my father."

I nod slowly. I was right about that, but she doesn't look me in the eye, and I wonder if there's more to it.

"Where are your guards?"

She bites her lower lip and looks up at me. It's the most adorable guilty kitten look, and my heart softens even though I know she's playing with me.

"I climbed over the wall yesterday," she admits.

"God damn, Isabella." I run my hands through my hair.

"Don't send me back." She grips the front of my t-shirt, and there's no faking the desperation in her eyes. "Please, Raiden. Don't send me back."

My name on her lips makes my dick ache. The scent of gardenias fills my nostrils and takes me back to that night two years ago.

My blood heats, and my cock twitches. I'm going to have sore balls tonight.

But the desperation on her face is all real. I've never known Isabella to beg before. Two years ago may have been the only time I've talked to Isabella, but that doesn't mean I haven't been keeping an eye on her. Watching her jog in the woods, following her to the climbing gym.

It was clear to me to see she was planning something; I don't know how Carlo didn't pick it up. But maybe he's not as observant of his daughter as she thinks he is.

My hand closes around hers, and I gently pry her fingers off my shirt.

"I won't send you back, Isabella, but you have to tell me the truth."

She nods and swallows hard. "You got anything to drink?"

I'm not letting her out of this room, so I go to the small fridge in the corner. It's full of beer and soft drink, and she chooses a Sunshine Squeeze apple juice.

WILD HEART

She takes her time opening it and swallowing a few large gulps. The drink seems to settle her, and when she's finished, she places the bottle carefully on the table.

She swishes her hair off her shoulders and sticks her chin out. The scared girl is gone, and the mafia princess is back.

My cock positively aches for her.

"I wanted to ruin my reputation," she says. "That's why I went to the strip club."

Her eyes are steady on me, and I believe her. "Why would you want to do that?"

"My father keeps me guarded because I'm his weakness. He thinks someone will snatch me because I'm such a prize. That's why I have no freedom." I nod, catching on. "Italians are an old-fashioned bunch. If I ruin my reputation, I lower my value. I am no longer such a prize."

"And you thought that would earn you more freedom?" It sounds like a stupid hare-brained scheme to me. But maybe that's how desperate she is. Isabella is wild and passionate; it must drive her crazy to have restrictions on her.

She raises an eyebrow. "I had to try."

"Why didn't you just run away? You got out of the estate somehow."

She looks away. "Because I couldn't do that to my

father. Despite it all, I love him, and I didn't want to never see him again."

She frowns, and I wonder what she's thinking about. If there's a soft side to Carlo that only his daughter and late wife have seen.

"Your father must be looking for you."

She sighs. "Yes. I'll have to go back eventually, but now my reputation is still intact." She gives me a flirtatious smile. "Unless you know anyone who wants to ruin it for me?"

A growl rumbles out of my chest. There's nothing I want more than to throw her on the table, rip off that ridicules skirt, and ravish her until she's screaming my name. To wipe that mask off her face and watch her come undone.

But she's Carlo Berone's daughter. That would be suicide.

"I won't send you home," I tell her. "You can stay here tonight until you figure out what you need to do."

Her shoulders sag in relief, but only for an instant before she pulls them upright.

"Thank you."

"I've got a room upstairs. You can shower, and I'll have food brought up. You're safe while you're here, Isabella. You have the club's protection. But the fewer people who know, the better if you don't want your father to find you too soon."

She smiles and throws her arms around me like a little girl, and I inhale her scent, my body responding to her sudden closeness.

"Thank you, Raiden."

She pulls her head back, and for the briefest moment her lips brush my cheek. It's an affectionate kiss, a thank you kiss. But the heat of her lips travels all the way down my body and straight to my cock.

I've invited a mafia princess to stay in my club, and I'm in big trouble.

8
ISABELLA

*R*aiden leads me out of the meeting room and up the stairs of his clubhouse. The low rumble of men's voices carries in from outside. Delicious smells waft down the corridor, and the sound of women's laughter comes from the kitchen.

"It's a club dinner tonight," he explains.

It's relaxed here, like a casual family gathering and nothing like the quiet tense halls of my father's estate.

Upstairs is a corridor with several doors leading off it, and he takes me to the one at the end of the hall. It's furnished plainly but comfortably with a large double bed and a bathroom adjoining it.

"This is my room when I need to crash. You can stay here."

The furnishings are navy blue and masculine. It

needs a woman's touch, but I'm grateful to have a place to stay.

Raiden strides to the bathroom and opens cabinets before returning with a bowl of hot water.

"Sit." He indicates an armchair near the bed.

I'm used to my father barking orders at me, and the defiance in me bubbles to the surface. I hate being told what to do, but Raiden holds up a medical kit and fixes me with a look that brooks no argument.

"I'm going to patch up your leg."

I'd forgotten about the scratch on my leg, and when I look down there's a trickle of blood on my shin. I sit in the chair, and he kneels before me with the bowl of hot water.

"Does the President of the club play doctor to all his guests?"

My father would never do this, get down on his knees before anyone. But Raiden wears his power with casual confidence. He doesn't need to prove anything to anyone.

"Only the pretty ones."

I roll my eyes at the easy compliment, because I don't want him to see how much it pleases me. I've been thinking about this man for the last two years. And even though I'm a mafia princess and used to compliments, the fact that he thinks I'm pretty has my tummy doing double flips like a schoolgirl.

Get a grip, Isabella.

"May I?"

Raiden indicates my leg with the scrape on it. He's polite, or maybe he knows no one touches a mafia princess without permission.

I nod, and his hand gently grips my shin as he lifts my leg to rest upon his knee. He studies the cut and I hold my breath, hoping he doesn't see the goosebumps that prick my skin at his touch.

"It's not deep," he says. "I'll clean it up and put a bandage on it."

His hands are rough, callused, and dirty with bike grease. I'm used to the carefully manicured hands of my father's associates. I can't pull my gaze away from his rough knuckles as he dips a towel in the bowl of water and brings it to my leg.

"This may sting."

He presses the towel to the cut, and the water going into the open wound stings like hell. I bite my teeth together to keep from flinching. My father brought me up to be strong, and I'm not about to cry over a tiny wound.

Raiden must notice my body tense, because he looks up at me and smirks.

"It's okay to feel pain, Isabella."

I keep my expression neutral. "I'm a Berone. I don't feel pain."

It's what my father would have the world think, but I'm teasing Raiden. He chuckles, and I can't keep my face straight.

It's nice to hear him laugh. Most people are scared of me and they don't get my deadpan humor, but this man sees into my very soul.

He's leaning so close to my leg that my skin prickles from the heat of his breath. I grip the sides of the armchair as the butterflies in my belly turn to something deeper. A tug in my core and a rising heat that makes me want to take his callused hand and slide it up my thigh.

He finishes cleaning the wound and reaches for a bandage. His breathing is ragged and he doesn't speak, and I wonder if he's feeling the same intensity of emotions that I am.

I've never been with a man before. I'm Catholic like my mother, and I'll not bed a man until I'm married to him. But so help me God, there are things I'd like this man to do to me that I can't explain. I'm not a sinner, but the way his fingers gently stroke my leg as he puts the bandage on and the heat in his eyes has me ready to go to the devil for what I need from him.

I drop my leg as soon as he puts the bandage on.

These feelings are too intense, too confusing. I'm a woman who likes to be in control, and what Raiden's making me feel has my mind and body in a whirl.

He stands up and reaches out a hand to me.

"Let's get that makeup off. I want to see your face."

I follow him to the bathroom. There's none of the expensive makeup remover that I'm used to. But when Raiden puts soap on a flannel, I don't care.

I sit on a stool as he instructs, enjoying being fussed over.

"Close your eyes."

I do as he says, and with a surprisingly gentle touch, he wipes across my eyes several times. It will be streaky and it'll probably cause a breakout, but I don't care. I've never been looked after in this way before. It reminds me of my mother wiping the mud off my face when I was a child.

"You still going by Trina?"

I open my eyes to find Raiden so close that I can see flecks of amber among the chocolate of his eyes. "Your fake name."

I laugh, remembering the fake ID I had made up to get into White Out. "No, Carmenta was what I used today."

"The Italian goddess."

I arch my eyebrow, impressed. "You know Roman mythology?"

"It would have been lost on those men."

There's a tightness in his voice, and a flash of anger crosses his features.

He's jealous.

The realization makes me smile. I thought he was treating me like a naughty child, but if he's jealous, then it means he *does* feel something for me.

I should tell him about my real reasons for running. Maybe he can help. But what could Raiden do against my father's wishes? It would bring a world of pain to his club. This is my own battle to fight.

"You can stay here for as long as you need."

Raiden runs the flannel under the tap, and a mix of colors wash into the sink. It's not a casual offer. He's putting himself at risk.

"My father might kill you."

It's not an idle threat but a fact. My father has a reputation for heavy handed justice.

"Nah." Raiden shakes his head casually. "I don't think so. Not if you're safe and happy, and it's your choice."

His gaze meets mine, and there's a flicker of hope.

He wants me to stay.

This powerful gruff biker who's more than twice my age wants me to stay here. My stomach flips, and even though I should be mad at this man for pulling me out of the strip club and ruining my plans, I find myself smiling like a dizzy schoolgirl.

I've blown my chance to foil my father's plans for me, but at least I can have a few days of freedom. To get to know the man who has haunted my dreams for the last two years.

Raiden bends down and wipes the flannel across my cheek, wiping away thick layers of foundation.

With him this close, I can smell his aftershave and bike oil. The scent makes my head feel light. My heart flutters with his closeness, and there's an ache between my legs that I long for him to ease.

I long to stay here with him, but I don't want to put anyone in danger.

"How about your club? My father might be…" Murderous? Vengeful? "…a little cross. I don't want to bring trouble to your club."

Raiden arches his eyebrow. "No doubt, Princess. I'll speak to the club because you're right. It's not just my ass I'm putting on the line. But I want you here, and no threat from your father will change that."

He looks so certain, the only man I've ever met not quaking at the threat of my father's anger.

His gaze darts to my lips and I part them, ready

for the kiss that his look promises. He leans forward and our eyes meet, my desire reflected in his.

I close my eyes, ready to feel his firm lips on mine. His breath tickles my lips.

There's a knock at the door, and my eyes fly open as Raiden pulls away.

"Fuck."

Raiden straightens up and runs a hand through his hair. He looks torn, and I hate that wanting to kiss me isn't enough. Is he scared of my father, or does he think I'm a little girl who can't handle him? Is he letting me stay because he wants me here or because his fatherly instinct is kicking in and he knows I'll be safe here?

I'll have to find a way to show him that I'm not a girl, that I'm all woman.

He strides to the door, and there's a woman on the other side. I haven't seen her before, but her smile is bright and her hair is pulled back in a cute 1950s do that matches her dress.

"I've brought some clothes and a plate of food."

"Thanks Danni."

Raiden takes the plate of food, and the woman drops the bag inside the door.

Her gaze finds mine, and she smiles sweetly, "I guessed you'd be about the same size as April."

Jealousy flares in me at the mention of another woman.

"You need anything else, just holler." Danni closes the door behind her, and I turn to Raiden.

"Who's April?" It comes out harsher than I intended, and Raiden chuckles.

"She's Snips's wife."

I turn away so he doesn't see my relief and *confusion.*

What is happening to me that this man makes me feel so much?

"I'll leave you to eat. There're fresh towels if you want a shower. Get some rest. I'll be right outside the door if you need me."

He shuts the door behind him, and I stare at it for a long time. We were so close to kissing a moment ago, and then he leaves abruptly.

Something's holding him back, and I intend to break down every one of his barriers.

9
RAIDEN

*B*arrel sways as he pulls out a chair around the long table and collapses into it. He makes a grab for Marcus's meat sandwich and Marcus pulls it out of the way, almost knocking over Arlo's beer.

"Watch it."

Arlo rescues his beer and proceeds to chug it back.

None of the men are pleased that I've called a meeting in the middle of a club dinner, but they don't complain. They know I wouldn't have called it if I didn't have to. Hell, I'd prefer if they were sober, but there's nothing I can do about that.

"Is this about the mafia princess you got stashed away upstairs?" Barrels looks smug as he says it. I cut a look to Marcus and Snips; they were the only ones who saw her come in.

They both shakes their heads.

"I didn't breathe a word, Prez." Marcus looks offended.

"Me neither," says Snips.

Barrels crosses his arms over his chest. "Come on, Prez, we're not blind. Even with your big hairy distraction here." He nudges Marcus, who puts on a front.

"What do you mean?"

I should have known better than to think I could sneak Isabella past my men. Barrels was special forces; he doesn't miss a thing. Even if he has been hitting the beer all afternoon.

I sigh and run my hands through my hair. I trust every man here, and they need to know who I've got upstairs and the consequences that it could lead to.

"Yes, Isabella Berone will be staying with us for a few days."

There're murmurs around the room, and I can tell from the pitch of them that not everyone's happy about our guest.

"Does her father know?" asks Travis.

I shake my head. "Not yet."

"Jesus." Travis shifts in his seat. "Are we gonna have a mafia hit squad after us?"

"Do we need to tool up, Prez?" Snips leans forward, looking excited. Some of my men miss their military days more than others.

"I hope not."

"But you can't be sure?" Barrels leans his giant elbows on the table. All trace of drunkenness has vanished. If I told my men to get ready for a shoot-out, they would. But I hope like hell it doesn't come to that.

"Carlo isn't going to come after our club. He's not that stupid."

There're grunts of dissent around the room. Not everyone agrees.

"I'm not keeping Isabella against her will. I rescued her from a... situation, and she's staying here for a few days."

There's raised eyebrows, but I'm not going into details.

"She was wearing your cut. Does that mean she's your old lady?"

I fix Arlo with a hard look, but the grin remains on his face.

I wonder how the hell he saw what she was wearing when I didn't even see him out back when we came in. Either my men are more observant than I give them credit for or they're massive gossips. Also I'm not answering any questions about what

Isabella is to me. She's mine, that's all I know. But until she knows it, I'm sure as hell not sharing that with my men.

"I heard she's bossy as hell," says Snips.

"The Prez has finally met his match," quips Travis.

The men break into lighthearted banter, but I can't deny anything they're saying.

"You're not stupid enough to deflower Carlo Berone's daughter are you, Prez?" asks Vintage. "Please don't do that. I don't want him to get all mafia on our asses. He'll likely take all of our balls, not just yours. And I'm quite fond of mine."

"I'm not de-flowering anyone." My voice chokes on the words, because that's exactly what I'd like to do to Isabella. But the men are right. I'm not that stupid.

"She's just here for a few days as our guest. Nothing more."

"We should send her back. We don't need that kind of trouble."

All eyes turn to the silent man in the corner with his arms folded. Specs doesn't speak much, and when he does it's thought out and the men respect him.

There're murmurs of ascent. But there's no way I'm sending my princess back. The only thing she'll be going back for is to pack her bags and kiss her daddy goodbye.

But I'm not admitting that to my men. Not yet.

"She's pretty," Davis adds.

Rage thunders through my body, and my fingers close into fists. Sensing the tension, the huge mastiff that follows him around sits up from her spot under the table by Davis's feet. Her tail thumps on the floor as I stare down Davis.

If it was anyone else but Davis, I'd rip their throat out for noticing her. But Davis is young. He got voted into the club from being a Prospect a few months ago. He doesn't know any better.

"Anyone lays a hand on Isabella, and I'll rip your balls out myself."

I thump my fist on the desk, and the room goes silent. The men are looking at me like I grew two heads. I make eye contact with each and every one of them so they know I'm serious.

"Prez has got it baaad," mutters someone from the back.

Geez, they can see right through me.

"We treat her as our guest, with respect. And she has our protection for as long as she's our guest."

"We voting on this?" asks Travis.

"No." I slam the gavel down. "There's no vote on

this. She's staying, and she has our protection. It's not negotiable."

I stalk out of the room and straight upstairs. Colter is sitting in the chair where I left him outside her door. He's one of top guys and about the only man I'd trust to guard Isabella right now.

"She come out?"

"No," he answers. "But I heard her singing."

Son of a bitch. He's heard her sing, and I want to rip his ears off for it.

"Go join the party," I tell him.

"You need anything, Prez? Food, beer?"

What I need is right behind that door.

I shake my head. "No. Go join your wife. I'm hanging here for a while."

Colter gives me a nod and heads back to the party. He doesn't ask questions and I give no answers. He'll get the low down from the men downstairs. Right about now, they'll be telling their wives about the mafia princess in the room upstairs and the entire place will be gossiping about it.

I don't care.

There's only one thing I care about right now. Making sure my princess doesn't leave here without knowing she's mine.

10

ISABELLA

I almost trip over the sleeping figure when I open my door the next morning. Raiden opens one eye and peers at me.

"Good morning."

He stretches and his t-shirt rides up, revealing the defined V-shape of his Adonis Belt and a hint of ink swirling around the side of his torso.

My mouth goes dry as I drag my eyes up to his. His hair's mussed up, and he's in the same clothes from last night.

"Have you been out here all night?"

He nods.

I don't want him to notice how pleased that makes me, so I hide it behind a scowl. "I've swapped one prison for another."

Raiden shakes his head. "You're free to go anytime you like."

I raise my eyebrows, because it sure as hell doesn't look like it if he's been standing guard outside my room.

"Then why did you spend the night here?"

He finishes his stretch and looks at me lazily. "Because if you're going to leave, I want the chance to convince you to stay."

I lean against the doorframe and study him closely, hoping he can't tell how pleased his words make me.

"So are you leaving?" His expression is causal, but apprehension flickers across it. He doesn't want me to leave.

"That depends." I let it hang in the air for a moment, enjoying watching him. "Do you serve breakfast downstairs?"

He stands up, and my gaze follows him as he draws himself to his full six foot something height. I'm not a small woman, but next to Raiden I feel petite. He takes a step toward me and his look is hungry, like I'm on the menu.

"What do you want, princess? Scrambled quail eggs? Pomegranates and cinnamon yoghurt?"

He's teasing me, and the smile that plays on his lips makes my core pull up tight.

"I eat regular food, you know. Poached eggs and hand caught wild Alaskan salmon will be fine."

He chuckles, and I like making him laugh. He holds his arm out for me, and I link mine through his as we walk downstairs.

The restaurant won't open for another couple of hours, and I sit at one of the tables while Raiden fetches cereal and milk and two bowls from the kitchen.

As we're crunching on Cheerios, he sits back and looks at me.

"So princess, what do you want to do today?"

I look out the window at the mountain road and the quiet valley beyond. It's so peaceful, made more so without the constant guards that follow me around.

I often wondered what it would be like to do normal things without my guard: go to a shopping mall, get my hair done without their presence. But there's really only one thing I want to do today.

"I want to go for another ride on the back of your bike."

Raiden raises his eyebrows, and I like that I've surprised him. But the bike ride last night was thrilling.

"I want to ride in the mountains where there are

no people. No one to recognize me. No one around at all."

Where it's just him and me, I want to add.

Raiden gives me a pleased smile. "Your wish is my command."

After breakfast, I grab a quick shower and meet Raiden out the back of the complex.

There's a group of men near the bike garage, and they nod at me as we walk past. They're respectful and friendly and not at all surprised to see me. It makes me wonder what Raiden said to them.

I slide onto the back of Raiden's bike and hook my arms around his waist. It feels natural to hold onto him like this, as if we were meant to fit together.

The bike roars to life, and a thrill zaps through me as we pull out of the complex.

Raiden takes us further up the mountain, expertly maneuvering around the winding mountain roads. Wind whips my hair behind me, and the cool breeze of the mountain road whips at my skin. It's exhilarating, riding like this. Like nothing else I've ever done, and I don't know if it's the thrill of the ride or the man on the bike in front of me.

. . .

Eventually we head down a dirt track and stop when it ends at a thicket of trees. There's a crumbling wooden post, the only indication of the overgrown path that leads through the trees.

"Come on."

Raiden takes a backpack out of his saddle bag and takes my hand in his. Our fingers link as we walk down the path.

The only sounds are the crunch of our footsteps, the rustle of leaves, and the birds singing around us. We speak quietly, talking like we've known each other for years. He tells me about life in the military and about the Wild Riders MC, becoming animated when he speaks about his club.

I tell him about my sheltered life, about losing my mother and life under my father's strict gaze at the villa.

It's peaceful, like I wanted, and for a moment, with this man holding my hand, I forget about where I am, who I am, and what my father is trying to make me do. For a while I'm just an ordinary girl, holding hands with a man who makes her stomach flip.

It feels like we've been walking for hours when we finally come to the end of the trail. It's a lookout right on the edge of the cliff, a rusty railing all that stands between us and the sheer drop of the cliff face.

The valley is spread out below us. Neat rows of pine trees decorate the slopes, and the only sign of humans is the sawmill in the distance.

"It's peaceful." I sigh contentedly. This is just what I needed. A break away from everyone.

"The other side of the hill is prettier," says Raiden. "Where the resort and the lake and Hope is. But if you want solitude and no tourists, then this is where to come."

"It's beautiful," I say, looking down at the valley.

"Sure is." When I look at Raiden, his gaze is on me. His eyes are full of heat as he takes a step toward me.

"Is this what you want, princess? Solitude?" His hand slides around my waist as he says it and I gasp, no longer able or willing to hide my feelings for him. "Is this the freedom you crave?"

His other thumb runs along my chin, the rough texture of his callused hand making my skin heat. How can I tell him that it's him I want? That wherever he is I'll be happy.

"It's a start."

His face is so close to mine that the heat of his breath skims my cheek as he chuckles.

"You're hard to please."

His eyes sparkle with mirth and desire, and it's a heady mix. All he has to do to please me is close the inches between us and press his lips to mine.

"I don't think I am."

I'm breathing hard as he dips his head. My eyes close as our lips meet. The kiss is firm, but his lips are soft. I sigh softly because it feels so right. This is freedom, right here, kissing this man.

He pulls away and looks down at me, and there's conflict in his expression.

"Stop worrying about my father."

He shakes his head. "I'm not scared of your father, Isabella."

"Then why are you holding back?"

"I'm old enough to *be* your father."

Relief floods me. Is that all he's worried about? "The age gap is nothing to me, Raiden."

My hand slides up his leg, and he groans as I press my palm against his hard bulge.

"See what you do to me, princess."

"I'm not a princess, Raiden. I'm a woman, and I demand that you touch me."

He chuckles. "Spoken like a true princess."

We're both smiling as our lips touch, and this time there's no hesitancy. His tongue forces entry, and I willingly comply. My body presses against his, and my core throbs with longing. I shudder against him as his hand slides up my leg.

This is what I've been waiting for. A man, this man, who's brave enough to kiss me.

Sensation floods my senses, and I whimper against him.

"Touch me, Raiden. I need you..."

His lips travel down my neck, and his breath is hot against my skin. "As you command, princess."

My eyes roll back in my head as his hands slide over my hips and to the front of my shorts. He undoes the button and slowly pulls the zipper down. My body's on fire and I want him to hurry up, but I'm not sure what it is I need him to do.

His fingers graze my panties, and then they're inside the flimsy fabric. I gasp as he slides through my slick folds, giving in to the sensation and letting his fingers work my body as his mouth devours mine.

He seems to know what I need without asking, expertly moving his fingers until I'm a bundle of nerves in his hand.

My back arches and my hair trails behind me like a waterfall. His hot kisses on my neck move to my breasts as his fingers keep strumming.

He doesn't try to enter me but rubs small circles until my sensitive nub can't stand it anymore.

"Raiden..."

I dig my nails into his forearms, holding on as my

body trembles beneath his touch. The cool air tickles my hot skin, and the sounds of insects fill my ears as his fingers work me into a frenzy.

My orgasm explodes inside me, and I come undone on his hand. I cry out, scaring birds into the air and disturbing the peace of the mountain. For one glorious moment, I'm free. My spirit lifts and my soul soars, shattering into a million pieces before coming back together.

I'm breathing hard as I stand myself upright.

Raiden slides his hand out of my shorts, and it's slick with juices. He brings his fingers to his mouth and sucks the juice off them.

"You taste delicious, princess."

My mouth drops open at the dirtiness of what he's just done. But it stirs something inside me and makes me want more. Raiden reaches for my shorts, and I think he's going to tug them off, but instead he zips them up and redoes the button.

I can't hide my disappointment.

"How about you?"

He cups my chin in his hand and kisses me hard on the lips. "We'll have plenty of time to take care of me later. But those clouds aren't hanging around."

I turn to see where he's looking, and thick rain clouds have rolled in over the valley.

"Come on."

I'm still shaking from what just happened as he clasps my hand and we set off down the trail. I can't hide the happy grin that spreads across my face. I've never let a man get even close to touching me like that. No man has ever been brave enough to attempt it. But Raiden's not scared of me or my father.

I feel safe with him and cherished. With Raiden, I truly do feel like a princess.

11
RAIDEN

There's nothing like riding your bike on a mountain road with a beautiful woman clinging to your back.

Isabella's warm hands wrapped around my waist make my chest swell. I love that she trusted me enough to come undone on my hand. It was the most beautiful sight I've ever seen, the stubborn princess giving in to my touch.

I want to do it again and again and again. And more, I want to claim her and make her mine for the entire world to see.

I'm not scared of her father, although I probably should be. Let him come. I'll fight his entire organization to be with my girl.

If that's what she wants.

I don't know if being with me is one more stunt

to shock her father. Isabella seems genuine but she's a complex woman, and there are secrets she's not telling me. I'm sure of it.

But as we slide off the bike and her leg brushes mine, I don't give a shit what she's hiding. As long as I can wrap those thick legs around me and bury myself inside her, to hell with whatever her father will do to me.

I'm not in the business of deflowering virgins for the fun of it. With Isabella, it's forever. I just need to convince her.

I take her hand in mine as we stride into the clubhouse. It's just after the lunch service, and the restaurant is full of customers. I don't want to take the chance of her being recognized, so we duck into the kitchen to grab a bite to eat.

Maggie's drizzling sauce over a thick slice of cake, and she looks up as we enter. She smiles when she sees Isabella.

"Are you hungry?" she asks shyly.

Maggie's our best pastry chef. She was shy as a mouse when she started working for us, but since she's been with Arlo, he's brought her out of her shell.

"Can you rustle us up some chicken or something? And a slice of whatever that is." I indicate the cake.

"Can do, Prez."

Arlo comes into the kitchen, and Maggie lights up when she sees him. He gives her a sultry kiss then nods to me, indicating he wants to talk. We step out of the kitchen, and I leave the women talking. Isabella's trying to help, and Maggie's too polite to shoo her out of the way.

"What's up?" I ask Arlo as soon as we're out of earshot.

"Carlo's looking for his daughter, and he's pissed. Word is he'll murder anyone who's helped her."

The words send a jolt of ice through my body. I like to think I'm not afraid of Carlo, but you'd be a fool not to have a little fear of the man.

Arlo tugs on his beard nervously. "You gonna send her back?"

I glance through the window to the kitchen. Isabella's holding the piping bag while Maggie instructs her on how to squeeze the icing out of it. Both women are laughing. I've never seen Isabella so relaxed. She likes it here.

A vision pops into my head of Isabella being around permanently, strutting through the clubrooms like she owns the place. Me and her as a team.

"No. I'm not sending her back."

Arlo takes a step backwards at the force of my words, and concern wraps around his face.

"Prez, her father's out of his mind. He thinks someone kidnapped her like they did his wife…"

I hadn't thought of that. Eliana, Carlo's wife, paid the ultimate price for her choice of husband. The man's had to deal with the grief ever since. It's got to be why he's such an uncompromising hardass and why he's so overprotective with his daughter. He must be fearing the worst.

"Have someone let it slip that she was seen boarding a bus on her own. Don't let it get traced back to us." The last thing I want to do is worry her father unnecessarily. "Put the poor guy out of his misery."

Arlo nods, but he doesn't leave. I get the feeling he wants to say more. He tugs on his beard, and I look at him expectantly.

"What is it?"

"You're going to have to face him sometime, Prez. You can't just keep her here without him ever knowing."

He says it gently, and I know he's right.

But I need more time. One more day to tie her to me for good.

"Don't let Isabella find out how upset her father is. We'll give her one more day of freedom."

"Then what? You gonna hand her back?"

There's no way I'm handing Isabella over to her

father. I need to tie her to me, but not by keeping her prisoner. It has to be her choice.

I have one more day. One more day to convince her she's mine.

"Not a chance."

Arlo shakes his head at me, but he's wearing a grin. "Love, Prez. It'll change your life."

We eat chicken salad and creamy chocolate cake on stools in the kitchen. I have some club business to do in the afternoon, and Isabella hangs out in my office. She's full of questions about the club, her natural curiosity and good business sense shining through. She even puts forward suggestions on how to expand our reach for distribution.

I listen to her, impressed. She's picked up a lot about business from her father. I wonder if he's planning on handing over the business to her one day. I hear mafia families are very traditional, but without a son, maybe that's what Isabella has been groomed for.

The thought makes me shudder. We run a legitimate business here, and I hate the thought of her doing anything else.

But when I ask, she laughs off the idea.

"You think I want to work with a bunch of old-fashioned Italian men? No way."

She looks offended that I'd even ask.

"Then what do you want to do, Isabella?"

She looks down, the first time I've ever seen her shy. I sit up in my chair, intrigued. "What's got my fiery princess tongue-tied?"

"It's stupid for the twenty-first century. I should want more."

I take her hand across the desk. "What is it? What does Isabella Berone, the Mafia princess want to do with her life?"

She takes a deep breath and looks up at me. "I want lots of babies."

It's not the answer I was expecting, and for a moment I just stare at her while my loins go into overdrive. I'll give her babies; I'll give her a whole damn house full.

"My mother only ever had me. She loved kids, and I want to be the kind of mother she was. I want a house full of children, and I'll be the best mother I can. That's all I've ever wanted."

She looks down again, embarrassed, but she doesn't realize how her confession has stirred me. I've already got a grown-up daughter. I thought that was enough. But with this woman, I suddenly see a future.

"I'll give you a baby." She laughs until she sees my expression.

"You're serious?"

I come around the other side of the desk and take her hands. "Come upstairs, and I'll show you how serious I am."

She pushes me away, laughing. "I'm a good Catholic girl, Raiden. I won't have sex until I'm married."

My eyes narrow. "You're telling me you're a virgin." It's what I hoped, but I long to hear her say it.

Her cheeks flush pink, and I love making my princess embarrassed.

"Yes, of course. And I will be on my wedding day."

I raise my eyebrows, but she's deadly serious. "How about what we did out there on the hike?'"

She shakes her head at me. "That wasn't sex, Raiden."

She's got a point. Technically, it wasn't. "Where do you draw the line about what you can do and what you can't do?"

All this talk has my blood running hot and my dick hard. She's breathing hard and I pull her up off the chair, clasping my hands around her waist.

"Why don't you spend the night with me and find out?"

My cock twitches, and I think I'm going to lose it in my jeans. This woman. She's not afraid to ask for what she wants, and the fact that she wants me has me hornier than a college boy.

I want to do all the things to her that she'll let me and then push her over the edge and do all the things she's denying herself, consequences be damned.

Without waiting another moment, I hoist her over my shoulder. Isabella squeals. I bet she's never been picked up like this in her life.

"Put me down." She thumps on my back, but I'm holding her too tight.

"We're going upstairs right now to find out how many orgasms I can give you while keeping your virginity intact."

She giggles as I carry her through the corridor and up the stairs.

We pass Marcus, and Isabella gives him a little finger wiggle as I carry her past. The Isabella of a few days ago would have rather died than have anyone see the way I'm manhandling her. But she just laughs, and the sound warms my very soul.

I make her happy. She's happy here.

With my arm clasped firmly around her thighs, I run up the stairs.

12

RAIDEN

I burst into the room and kick the door shut behind me with my foot. Reaching back, I lock the door, then carry Isabella to the bed. I throw her down a little rough, and she bounces up to her elbows looking at me with fire in her eyes.

"You carried me like a rag doll," she accuses.

"Did you like it?"

She parts her lips, and her eyes fill with desire. I lunge for the bed just as she sits up and we meet in the middle, our lips colliding as our bodies press together.

My urgency is matched with her own as we tear at each other's clothes. Her teeth bite my lips and her hands rove over me, tugging off my jacket then my shirt. It's urgent and passionate, and we're both breathing hard when we come up for air.

Her thick hair is sticking up around her face, and her lip gloss is smudged. She's never looked so beautiful, and I can't help the grin that spreads across my face.

"What are you grinning for, Prez?" Her eyes narrow in suspicion.

"I'm thinking about all the ways I can make you come without fucking you."

Her eyes widen, and her mouth drops open. I kiss her swollen lips as my hand cups her breast. I slide off the rest of her clothes until she's naked on the bed, sitting back on her haunches.

She's beautiful, curvy and unashamed of her body. There're dark hairs on her arms and little ones coating her belly.

I go to push her gently back on the bed, but she shakes her head.

"You're not getting me on my back, biker."

I like that she's got as much sass completely naked as she does fully clothed.

"How else am I going to lick your pussy?"

Her eyes widen, and she moans as my hand slides between her legs. My fingers come out slick and sticky with her juice.

"You lie down," she commands. "I want to be on top."

I chuckle, but it doesn't surprise me that Isabella

wants to be in control. It's fine by me. A nasty thought goes through my head making me tense.

"Have you done this before?"

Her eyes narrow. "What do you take me for? No, Raiden. Besides the fact that I've never had an opportunity, I've never met a man I wanted to do this with."

Her eyes meet mine, and in that moment I see her vulnerability and her passion. There's a thing between us that can't be stopped, and she feels it too. It defies our age gap and status and who we are.

There's raw emotion in my voice when I speak.

"I'll take care of you, Isabella." She thinks I mean sexually, but I mean for the rest of her life. With all that I am and all I can offer, I'll take care of her in all the ways a man takes care of a woman.

This time when we kiss, it's softer. Less urgent. Our bodies move together, and I let her push me down onto the bed.

My cock's sticking straight up and she bends to it, but I pull her up so she's straddling my chest. "I want to taste you, Isabella. Climb on up here, princess."

Without a moment's hesitation, she shuffles upwards so her thighs are positioned on either side of my face. The musky scent of her arousal fills my nostrils, and I place a hand on each ass cheek as I pull her down onto my ready mouth.

She moans as I lap at her dripping pussy. My senses go into overdrive as I taste her, caress her and breathe her in, making me feel more alive than I have in years.

"Raiden…"

She gasps and her hips pitch forward. She grasps the headboard as I explore her virgin pussy with my tongue.

She's not nervous or flirty. Like a true princess, she settles on my face, rocking back and forth, taking what I'm giving her as if it's her God damn right. And it is. I'll spend the rest of my life with Isabella riding my face if that's what she commands.

She leans back, stretching her arms up to catch her hair above her head, her body writhing as she enjoys herself on my tongue. It's a beautiful sight, and no matter what happens between us, one that will be etched on my memory forever.

She reaches back, and her hand clasps around my cock.

I groan into her as her delicate hands slide up my length.

She gives me a couple of blissful tugs then sits back up, positioning herself over my mouth like she was born to ride me.

"Faster," she gasps, even now trying to control the pace of my tongue.

I do as she commands, loving the moans that come out of her. Her fingers pinch at her nipples, and I'm going to lose it just watching her enjoy herself.

She presses herself against my face, taking everything I have, until my head is deep in the pillow. I could suffocate here a happy man as long as she takes what she needs from me.

She moans my name as her climax builds, the soft cries getting louder the closer she gets to release.

Suddenly she leans forward, and her body tenses. A string of Italian curse words spill out of her mouth, and her pussy convulses as her juice coats my tongue.

I hold her to me until the flutters of her pussy walls cease. Then I move my tongue again until I draw a second orgasm out of her. She shudders on top of me, her fingers gripping the headboard so tight her knuckles turn white.

When she moves this time, I let her dismount. But I'm not done with her yet.

She looks sleepy and adorable, and I give her a long kiss.

"Turn around," I growl.

She does what she's told, to my surprise, and I

make a mental note. If I want Isabella Berone to obey me, then two orgasms should do it.

When she's turned around, I grab her hips and pull her ass back to me.

"This time you're going to taste my cock, princess."

She has a sharp intake of breath at my dirty words, but I don't give her time to protest. I push her down on all fours as I slide a finger between her wet folds.

She lands with her hands on either side of my thighs in the perfect position.

"I've never done this before, Raiden."

My cock twitches. I'm about to explode from her hot breath on my dick and knowing her innocent mouth is about to be claimed.

"Good," I say. "I'll be the first and the last cock you'll ever have in your mouth."

I plunge my tongue into her pussy, not giving her time to respond. She gasps, and then I feel the sweetest heat wrap about my cock as her swollen lips ease down my shaft.

I groan into her pussy, wondering how the fuck I got so lucky. Then all thought flees my mind as her inexperienced mouth fumbles with my cock. She licks and sucks, and her teeth nip at my sensitive skin.

She only gags once, and then like a good princess, Isabella Berone opens her jaw and takes my cock all the way down her virgin throat.

I grip her hips as pleasure fills every part of my body. My nerve endings zing with energy, and my balls pull up tight.

As she gains confidence her moves become quicker, racing me towards my peak. I should pull back, but I want to claim her today, to let loose inside her. I want her to know she's mine.

It takes all the willpower I have to hold off until she comes again. As she does she sucks hard, and the vibrations of her muffled cries reverberate around my cock, detonating my release. I cum hard, a full load, all the way down her throat. Isabella coughs and splutters, but like a good girl she keeps her lips firmly clamped around me.

It's not until I'm fully spent that she releases her sweet hold. She turns around, and I scoop her into my arms.

"How did I do?"

"Not bad for a virgin."

She swats me playfully.

"The next time I cum inside you, Isabella, it will be in your pussy when you're my wife."

She rolls her eyes and tsks at me. She thinks I'm joking, but I couldn't be more serious.

This is the woman I want by my side for the rest of my life.

Her eyes are droopy, so I don't push it for now. Instead, I scoot the sheets down and we crawl into bed. She lies on her side and my body wraps around hers, shielding her from whatever would do her harm.

She's mine now. And tomorrow I'll make sure she knows exactly what that means.

13

ISABELLA

There's a warm body pressed against me, and I snuggle into it. Raiden's heavy arm drapes over my hip and I pull it up to my chest, loving the warmth that spreads through me at his touch.

But it's more than that. This is the first time in my life that I've woken up feeling truly free.

Yesterday I did something I wanted to. I spent the day with the man I've been dreaming about for two years.

I was worried he was thinking of me only as a daughter, but last night proved that's not the case. With Raiden, I feel like a woman. A confident woman. Not someone to be hidden away and kept under guard because she might break.

His fingers brush against my breast, and I gasp as

he finds my nipple. It only takes one touch from him and my body heats, ready for him. I long to feel Raiden inside me, but I made my vows in front of God. I'll stay a virgin until my wedding day.

But it doesn't mean we can't have some fun.

His hardness pushes into me and I wiggle my hips, making him groan.

"I want you so bad, princess."

It would be so easy to spread my thighs and guide him into my heated pussy. But I also like the challenge of denying myself. Of not giving him everything he wants.

"It's not possible."

I roll over, but I can't hide the grin on my face. My hands clasp his cock, and I take it in both hands.

"But I haven't made you come with my hands yet, biker."

He groans, and his eyes scrunch up like he's in pain. I enjoy watching this powerful man come undone.

I'm not sure what I'm doing with my hands, but I trust that Raiden will let me know if I do something wrong, and by the way he's groaning I think I'm doing it all right.

His hand slides between my legs as his lips meet mine. It's slower this morning, tender, and I let the feelings wash over me as we pleasure each other.

I could get used to this, waking each morning with this man by my side.

Raiden slides a finger into me, and it's so intense that I almost lose it. He chuckles and applies pressure to my clit with his palm.

It doesn't take long until the orgasm shakes through my body. But he doesn't let up, not until I've come three times. I stroke his cock hard, wanting him to have his release too.

"I wish I could be inside your tight pussy, princess."

He's full of yearning and it would be so easy to give in, but I tsk at him and shake my head.

"That is a privilege reserved for my husband."

He groans and I pick the up the pace, tugging hard with both my hands.

In another moment he tenses, and thick ropes of cum spurt out of his dick and coat my fingers. He lies back with a contented sigh and pulls me toward him.

"Was that okay for my first hand job?"

Raiden chuckles. "Princess, that was amazing. You're amazing." He sits up in bed and pulls me onto his lap. "So amazing that there's something I want to ask you."

He brushes a strand of hair off my cheek and

tucks it behind my ear. His expression is serious and I tense, wondering what's coming.

"Isabella Berone, will you marry me?"

My heart stills at his words. Then it jump starts when I realize what he wants. I push him away.

"You just want inside of me, Raiden."

I slide out of bed, but he grabs hold of my wrist. "I'm being serious, Isabella. I don't want to marry you so I can fuck you. Although..." his gaze sweeps over my naked body, "...that does have some appeal. I want to marry you because I'm in love with you."

My heart skips a beat at his words. Words I've been longing to hear. I turn to look at him, and his expression is sincere, hopeful.

"Don't play with me, Raiden."

He reaches for something in the bedside drawer and pulls out a small box. He flips the lid open, and there's a ring inside. A giant emerald surrounded by diamonds.

"This is how serious I am, Isabella. It's a serious question. I love you; will you be my wife?"

My hand flies to my chest. The ring is beautiful, but... "When did you get this?"

Raiden's gaze flicks to the ring and back to me. "I bought it right after the night I met you at the club two years ago. I knew then you'd be my wife,

Isabella, I just needed to give you time to grow up and realize it yourself."

I stare at him with my mouth hanging open. Because it's everything I wanted since I met him too. I thought he would think I was a troublesome girl. I thought he'd be scared of my father. But Raiden isn't scared of anyone. It's what I want, to spend the rest of my life with this man.

"Yes," I say. "Yes, yes, yes!" I throw my arms around his neck, and we're both laughing as I shower his face with kisses.

"Emerald to match your eyes." Raiden slips the ring on my finger. "But before we tell anyone, I need to speak to your father."

At the mention of my father, the smile slides off my face.

"He won't be happy."

"It's your happiness I care about, princess. But I have to do the honorable thing."

He's going to be angry. He had plans for me. Plans that I need to tell Raiden about. The reason I ran away.

I open my mouth to speak when there's a knock at the door.

"Go away," Raiden grunts.

The knock comes again. "Sorry, Prez." There's an

urgency in the man's voice that makes Raiden look up. "Carlo Berone is downstairs."

14
RAIDEN

Carlo is seated at a table in the middle of the empty restaurant. A man stands on either side of him, a few feet behind. Far enough away to give the illusion of privacy, close enough to be deadly if I make the wrong move.

Arlo places a steaming cappuccino in front of him, and Carlo gives him a tight smile.

"Thank you."

His manners are impeccable, like the Italian suit he's wearing, tailor made to his large frame. He takes his time lifting the streaming cup to his lips and drinks.

"Ahhh, this is good coffee, Raiden."

He speaks without looking at me, and it's not until I pull out the chair opposite him and sit down that his gaze shifts to mine.

Carlo Berone is as frightening up close as the rumors say he is. His face is heavy set with deep lines furrowing his brow. He's about the same age as me, but the worry lines make him look older. His dark eyes are as intelligent as his daughter's, but with none of the sparkle. As they bore into me, I stare straight back.

I won't be intimidated by this man, not in my own clubhouse.

"I take it you're not here for the coffee."

Carlo sets the cup down and the scrape of crockery is the only sound in the place.

"No, Raiden. I'm here for my daughter."

The genial smile goes from his face, and when he looks at me again there's barely veiled animosity.

I'm not going to insult him by pretending she's not here. It was only a matter of time before she was traced to the clubhouse. Someone must have seen her on the back of the bike, and there's only one MC on Wild Heart Mountain.

"What if she doesn't want to go back?"

Carlo eyes me warily, and I get the feeling I'm being assessed. That he's trying to figure out what kind of man I am.

"You have a daughter."

He says it softly, and my heart drops to my stomach. I push back my chair, and his men step forward. "If you've done something…"

He raises a hand, stopping the men and making me pause. "Relax. I'm not in the business of hurting little girls. I merely bring up your daughter because you understand how much I love mine. How she's the most important thing in the entire world to me."

I keep staring at him, but I don't sit down. I'm not sure if he brought up Charlie as a threat, but if he mentions her again, I'm ready to tear his heart out.

Then I remember this is my future father-in-law. For Isabella's sake, I need to do this right.

Forcing a tight smile, I sit back down.

"Daughters are precious."

"Yes," he agrees. "Which is why I need mine back in my house, where I know she's safe."

"What if Isabella doesn't want to go?"

Carlo takes a deep breath. "I have powerful enemies, Raiden. And powerful men know that their women are their weaknesses. Isabella is a target. As was my late wife."

He swallows hard at the mention of his wife, and I wonder if the old crime boss has a heart after all.

"I will not let my enemies get to my daughter. I have ways of keeping her safe. Plans that will ensure her safety in the future."

His hand forms a fist on the table, the only indication of how agitated he is.

A surge of empathy flares inside me. It must be horrendous to fear your daughter will be taken. But Isabella can't live her life behind bars. And not when that life is with me.

"I can keep her safe."

Carlo tilts his head and regards me. He must read something in my expression, because his look softens. "You love her."

He says it matter-of-factly, no emotion, and I wonder what he thinks of a man the same age as he is being with his daughter.

"Yes," I say simply. "I'm going to marry her."

Shock flashes across his face and then it's gone, replaced by a neutral expression.

"And I suppose this was her idea?"

I shake my head. I don't think it was, only that she's withholding sex until she's wed, but even without that incentive, I was going to make her my wife someday.

"No. I proposed this morning, and she accepted. We'd like your blessing."

His lips turn up in a smile, and a low chuckle rumbles out of his throat.

"The little minx is cleverer than I thought."

He looks down and shakes his head, amused. I

don't know what's so funny, and I get the feeling I'm missing something.

"Explain."

Carlo looks at me, and now there's pity in his expression.

"I'm sorry, Raiden. It looks like she's played you."

I don't like being left out of the joke, and I reach across the table and grab him by the lapels. His men spring forward, but Carlo speaks rapid Italian and they pause.

"Tell me what the fuck you mean."

"Okay, but I hate to be the one who breaks your heart."

What he's saying doesn't make sense. He's talking as if Isabella has been using me, but that's not the case. Everything we've shared is real.

I think.

I let go of his lapels. "Talk."

"I suppose she told you about the marriage I arranged for her?"

My brain's in a spin. I don't know what he's talking about. Carlo must sense my confusion, because he continues.

"A married woman is less of a target then an innocent maid. She loses her value as a hostage once she is married, especially if she's married to another powerful family. Once Isabella is married to Rocco

Moretti, she will have the protection of two families. Anyone crossing me will also cross the Moretti family. Some of my enemies might be stupid enough to take me on, but to take on the Berones and the Morettis? No one is that stupid."

The blood pulses in my ears. Isabella is promised to someone else. Why didn't she tell me.

"She obviously doesn't want to marry this Rocco guy."

Carlo smiles. "No, she's made that clear. She doesn't like the boy. But it's the best thing for her. You understand that sometimes fathers have to make difficult choices to protect their daughters."

"But she's marrying me now."

Blood courses hot through my veins, and my hands form fists under the table at the thought of my Isabella being married off to someone else.

"Yes. Clever minx. If she's already married, I can't force her to marry Rocco."

I stare at him, trying to keep my expression neutral while my heart splits in two.

"I suppose she had you believe she was in love with you? My daughter has a way of making people think that. You've known her, what? Two days, Raiden? Do you think love works that quickly?"

My mind races over the past two days. Every look we shared, every smile, every time she fell apart under my touch. Could she have been faking all of it?

I run a hand through my hair. Carlo looks sorry for me, and I want to wipe the smug look off his face, tell him it isn't true. But is it? Everything I thought we had, the future I've been imagining comes crumbling down around me.

"I'm sorry, Raiden. Isabella is cunning and manipulative. She learned it from me. I'm dangerous, but those qualities in a beautiful woman are deadly."

I squeeze my eyes shut, remembering her scent, the softness of her lips and the way her eyes shone when I told her I loved her. It's got to be real; it's got to.

I stand up so quickly the chair clatters to the floor behind me. I have to see Isabella; I have to look her in the eye and find the truth.

15
ISABELLA

I pace the room, staying put like a good girl, like Raiden asked me to. But it's taking too long, and I need to find to out what's going on. I pull open the door just as Raiden stalks down the corridor.

"Is it true?"

I step backwards into the bedroom as he stomps into my space, his body tense and demanding, forcing me backwards with the force of his anger.

One look at his face, and I know that he knows about Rocco.

"Are you engaged to Rocco Moretti? Did you run away to get out of the marriage?"

There's no point in denying it. I should have been honest from the start. "My father arranged the marriage. They decided that we were engaged, but I never consented."

The anger rolls off him in waves, and it's frightening. Raiden has always been calm; I've never seen him so tense. I didn't think he'd be this cross when he found out.

"I ran away because if I stayed, I would have been forced to marry. I wanted to sully my reputation so the Moretti family didn't want me."

"That's why you chose the Fuzzy Peach strip club."

"Yes. If I worked there long enough, word would get out and I wouldn't be a suitable match."

It seems like a stupid plan now, but I was desperate. I couldn't run away and leave my father. But I couldn't marry a man I didn't love either.

"And I came along and ruined your plans," he mutters.

It's true. He did. But I don't regret it. The last few days have been the best of my life, and he saved me from going through with my hare-brained scheme.

"And so I became the target, your way out."

I'm taken aback by what he says. Does he think this isn't real? By the hurt look in his eyes, he does. "What has my father been telling you?"

"That you're smart, and you realized if you were already married you wouldn't have to marry Rocco."

The audacity of it makes me suck in my breath.

"And you believed him?"

By the anger and hurt on Raiden's face, I know the answer. After everything we shared, after the intimacy of the last few days, he thinks I would do that to him.

"You think I was faking my feelings for you?"

Anger bubbles up inside me. How deep is his love for me if he thinks I would do something like that to him, and how dare my father put such nonsense in his head.

The anger ignites something in me. My blood heats, and anger flares in my eyes.

"You men always think you can control me. You think I would swap one loveless marriage for another? You think I don't have a heart with feelings? That I don't want to be loved? You think you can decide who I marry without giving me a choice?"

At least Raiden has the good grace to look sheepish. He backs up as I stalk toward him, but I'm so angry at him my finger digs into his chest with every point.

"Do you think I would say yes and marry you if I didn't want to? My father thinks he controls me. But the truth is I would never go through with that marriage. If we were in the church, I would say no when the priest asked. But that would embarrass my father. I thought it was better if the Moretti family called it off, if they thought I was unsuitable. I won't agree to something as sacred as marriage unless it's my choice."

The fight has gone out of Raiden's expression, and now he looks miserable.

"You think I said yes to you so I wouldn't be able to marry someone else? It's not true. I said yes because I've been in love with you ever since I saw you in the club that night. For two years, I've waited to grow up enough to be the kind of woman you need by your side. For two years, I've thought about you every time I went to bed. I've dreamed about you. I've touched myself thinking about you. I said yes because I don't want to live another day without you by my side. I said yes because I love you."

We're both breathing hard, and he cups my hand in his cheeks.

"Isabella, I never knew… Why did you never call me? You had my number?"

"Because I wasn't ready. I didn't think you'd be interested in a girl. And I didn't want you to save me. I wanted to save myself."

He chuckles and presses his lips to mine.

"My fiery princess. You don't need saving from anything."

"My father thinks differently. He sees enemies in every shadow, and I don't know if he's right to be cautious or if he's paranoid because of my mother's death. I don't know if he'll ever let me be free."

I slump against Raiden, and he wraps his arms around me.

"He loves you too much." Raiden kisses the top of my head. "He's downstairs. Let's see him together and tell him that we're still getting married."

My heart feels heavy. I don't know how my father will take it, but if I have to choose, I choose Raiden every time.

We head downstairs, and I find my father admiring the vintage bike on the wall while a bearded man who I think is called Vintage tells him all about the parts. My father seems genuinely interested, and I stop short to watch him talking with the man. In another life he could be happy with the simple things, good coffee and conversation.

When he sees me, he smiles in relief and envelopes me in his big arms.

"Isabella, I was so worried."

His look tells me we'll discuss it more in private, but the relief on his face is real.

His gaze darts to where I'm clasping Raiden's

hand, and a flash of surprise goes through his features.

"We're getting married, Papa, and you can't stop us." I stick my chin out defiantly. "And before you talk any more nonsense, it's because we're in love, not because I'm trying to get out of marrying Rocco Moretti. You can give us your blessing or we can run away, but either way we're doing this."

Papa sighs heavily, and his beady eyes look Raiden up and down.

"Isabella will have the full protection of the club. We may not be mafia, but we're trained military men and our chapter is strong. Anyone fucks with us, they fuck with the entire Wild Riders MC throughout the state and any other veterans on the mountain."

As he talks, the other men from the club come up behind him. I recognize Marcus and Arlo and other familiar faces whose names I don't know yet. Each of them gives me a nod of support, a silent pledge to protect me as their own.

The women come to stand by their men, some of them holding babies on their hips. Each one gives me a nod as she accepts me into the club.

Warmth spreads through me at the acceptance I've found here. Raiden squeezes my hand and I blink quickly, fighting back the tears that threaten to sting my eyes.

I've got a family here. A support group of men and women who will ensure no real or imaginary harm comes to me.

My father sees it too, because he looks at the group gathered behind Raiden and he nods slowly.

"All right, Raiden. I give you my blessing to marry my little girl."

The last words come out choked, and Papa turns away quickly. I fling my arms around him and squeeze him tight.

"Thank you, Papa," I whisper into his ear.

He bats me off, and I know it's because he doesn't want to appear weak. But he's not fooling anyone.

There's a popping noise, and both my father's men draw their guns. Everyone freezes, and Arlo's voice comes from behind the bar.

"It's just champagne. I didn't mean to start a gunfight."

The men relax, and there's nervous laughter. Arlo hands around glasses of champagne, and Raiden pulls me to him. Our bodies press together, and he hardens against me.

"Let's make it a short engagement," he murmurs into my ear.

I couldn't agree more.

EPILOGUE

ISABELLA

Two weeks later…

The wedding bells ring out, signaling the end of the service. I haven't stopped grinning since I met my husband at the top of the aisle fifteen minutes ago.

The chaste veil does nothing to hide the flames that burn under my skin as his hands clasp mine.

We turn to face our guests, and Raiden allows me exactly three seconds before he practically drags me up the aisle.

I'm going as fast as my six inch white satin heels will take me, smiling at well-wishers as we go. Raiden has a scowl on his face, and he slows down for no one as he pulls me out into the sunshine.

Chiara and Alessia smile broadly at me. I've been

forgiven for giving them the slip, and I convinced my father to keep them on. They'll stay in the household for whenever I visit.

"Congratulations, signora."

Alessia smiles and steps forward hesitantly. I pull her in for a hug. She's wearing her dark hair twisted into an elaborate plait and makeup coats her cheeks.

"Come on, wife." Raiden growls and tugs at my hand "Before the whole goddamn congregation catches up with us."

I give him a look of mock horror. "Do not take His name in vain in a chapel."

"We're not in the chapel now, princess, and if you're not careful I'm going to take you in the chapel right in front of all our guests and the priest."

I giggle, but the strained look on his face makes me think he might be serious.

We start off across the garden, ignoring the cheers from our guests.

I turn back to see Marcus coming out of the chapel with his phone pressed to his ear and a scowl on his face. Raiden notices too, and Marcus looks up and catches his eye. Raiden pauses, but only for an instant.

"If that's club business, he'll have to figure it out himself," he mutters.

Marcus gives Raiden a small shake of his head and turns away to take the call.

"It's probably that art collector who was hanging around Danni's studio," I say.

Raiden frowns. It's the last thing on his mind, and I make a note to tell him about it later. They bought a couple of Marcus's wood carvings and want him to do a feature for some magazine, but Marcus isn't interested.

"Where are you taking me?" It rained last night, and with every step my heels sink further into the grass.

"To the first place I can find to claim you as my wife."

I stop as my shoe squelches in the ground, making it hard to walk.

Raiden growls impatiently. "Leave it behind."

He lifts me up and my left foot comes right out of the shoe, leaving it in the garden like Cinderella. There're whoops from the guests behind us, and I turn to them as Raiden carries me the rest of the way across the garden.

Charlie, Raiden's daughter, stalks to the front of the crowd. Even from across the garden, I can tell her eyes are narrowed as she watches us. She doesn't approve of her father's choice of wife. Not that she's said as much, but she doesn't have to. Ever since she turned up three days ago, I've had the distinct impression that she doesn't like me. Maybe because I'm three months younger than her and she thinks it all happened too fast. That no one can fall in love as quickly as we did.

Probably just because she hasn't found love yet.

Barrels comes up to talk to her and she turns to him. A rare smile lights up her face, and I wonder what the man could have possibly said to make her laugh.

I'll have to work on that relationship, but for now it's my husband I'm thinking of as he carries me through the high walls of the renaissance garden.

He sets me down on one of the benches and slides my other shoe off. The scents of lavender and rosemary are heavy in the air and bees buzz nearby, making the air seem hazy.

"You deserve a bed of roses for your first time, princess, but I can't wait any longer."

He nestles between my thighs, and I raise my legs to clench them around his waist. He groans as I pull him toward me.

"I can't either."

Our lips collide, and our bodies clash together as the urgency overtakes us. I've been waiting two weeks for this moment. Two agonizing weeks. We've done all sorts of things to each other but never gone all the way.

Now, my body yearns to feel Raiden inside me, to have my husband claim me as his.

He hikes up my wedding dress, pulling at fabric as it rips under his fingers. But we don't stop. The delicate lace of the veil catches on the wall behind us, and I tug it off my head. It was my mother's, and I don't want it damaged. But the rest of the dress I don't care about.

"You think anyone will come for us?" I ask between kisses.

"Not if they know what's good for them."

His kisses move down my throat as his hands tug at my panties. There's the sound of ripping satin, and they come away in his hand.

My fingers work at his belt, and Raiden groans as my hand encloses his stiff length. He lifts my hips, tilting me to find the angle we need.

"You ready, wife?"

His voice is choked, ragged with lust. My gaze finds his, and in the frenzy of our need, we pause as our eyes lock.

Love flows between us, raw and true and strong. I'm glad I waited for this moment, until we truly belonged to each other.

"I'm ready, husband."

With a hard thrust, Raiden is inside me. There's scorching pain, and I gasp as my fingers dig into his shoulder.

Then it eases as he moves with me, and I feel every ridge of his beautiful cock. It's pure bliss, unbelievable pleasure, more fulfilling than I ever thought possible.

We're both gasping as he pistons into me, the pleasure welling up inside me until I can't stand it anymore.

"Raiden," I cry out, forgetting that our wedding guests are on the other side of the wall.

"Good, princess. Let them know who you belong to."

I scream his name as he draws me to ecstasy and over the edge.

There's the sound of cheering from our guests. I should care, but I don't, and when Raiden moves in faster thrusts, I come again, not caring who hears us.

This time he shudders with me, and I feel his hot release shoot into the back of my womb. Maybe this will be the start of our first child.

I offer a silent prayer for it to be so.

When we're both spent he withdraws, and sticky cum slides down my thighs. A reminder that I belong to him that I'll keep under my dress all night.

We're both breathing hard as we rest our foreheads against each other.

"I love you, wife," Raiden says, and the new moniker makes me hot all over again.

"I love you too, husband."

We both grin, and his hand captures my waist.

"We'd better get back to our guests," I say.

"Not just yet." He's got a mischievous look about him as he spins me around and presses me against the wall. Cool air hits my butt as he hikes up my wedding dress.

"Be good for your husband, princess."

His words make my pussy heat and I bend over, showing him how ready and needy I am. I flick my hair over my shoulder and he grabs hold of it, wrapping it around his fist. My neck draws back just as his cock enters me.

I gasp at the sensation, at how deep he goes. My cheek brushes the wall, scraping dirt and rubbing off my wedding makeup.

I'm supposed to be the perfect bride today, but instead I'm a dirty wife. And I love it.

* * *

BONUS SCENE

Find out what family life looks like for Isabella and Raiden when this mafia princess becomes queen of the MC.

Read the Wild Heart bonus scene when you sign up to the Sadie King mailing list.

To get the bonus scene visit:
authorsadieking.com/bonus-scenes

Already a subscriber? Check your last email for the link to access all the bonus content.

WHAT TO READ NEXT

She's the city girl looking for a story. He's the grumpy mountain man hurting from his past...

Only bad things happen on Valentine's Day, and this year looks to be no exception.

I've been sent to the middle of nowhere mountain to write a story on a reclusive ex-military artist who doesn't want to talk.

My job's on the line, I've got a pile of debt, and Mom needs me back in the city. But if I don't get Marcus to talk, I'm fired.

I've seen the way he looks at me, and I'm not above using my feminine curves to lure the mountain recluse out of his lair.

But once he's out, I might not want to put him back in.

As long as he doesn't find out what I'm really up to...

Wild Valentine is a grumpy/sunshine, city girl/mountain man, forced proximity instalove romance featuring a scarred ex-military hero and the innocent curvy girl he makes his Valentine.

WILD VALENTINE

EXCERPT

Marcus

The warbly notes of Celine Dion blast through the speaker behind the bar as Davis preps for the morning shift.

I usually don't mind that he has the radio turned up way too loud. The poor kid lost half his hearing, but why the fuck does every station have to play sappy love songs just because it's fucking Valentine's Day next week?

"Can you turn that shit off?"

Davis gives a wide grin. "What's the matter, Wood, not a fan of Celine?"

Not a fan of love more like it, but I'm not going to get into that with Davis. He's young. He'll learn in his own time that love is an illusion, and women can't be trusted.

Davis turns the volume down, thank God, just as Calvin strides in, or Badge as we call him on the road.

His Sheriff's uniform is crumpled, and there's dark stubble on his usually smooth jaw.

"Double expresso," he says to Davis as he leans on the bar with his head in his hands.

"Trouble in town, Sheriff?"

Badge lets out a long sigh. "Just another bachelorette party."

Davis raises his eyebrows as he slides the steaming expresso cup toward Badge.

"Doesn't sound too bad, Sheriff."

Badge eyes the younger man warily. I'm sure to a twenty-something year old breaking up unruly bachelorette parties sounds like a wild time, but Badge is about the same age as me, thirty-four, and just as weary of women.

"They're wilder than the men some of them," he says. "And when you're responsible for the safety of those women on the mountain, it's no fun at all. Not when half of them are determined to get themselves into some kind of trouble."

"What was it this time?" I ask with mild amusement.

"They were getting rowdy by the lake. There were complaints from guests at The Lodge. They were so drunk on fruity cocktails not one of them would listen to me."

I chuckle despite myself, imagining Badge trying to tame a group of drunk women. He's a good looking guy and probably got propositioned by more than one.

"Had to get Axel to help me escort them back to their rooms. One of them was missing, and we spent the entire goddamn night looking for her. Turned out she'd fallen asleep in a batch of poison ivy. I've just come back from dropping her at the medical center in Hope. Goddamn bachelorette parties shouldn't be allowed."

I chuckle at my friend and MC brother, but he takes his job seriously. He really does feel responsible for those women.

"Is Prez in?" he asks.

I shake my head. We haven't seen much of the Prez since his honeymoon. Poor man's gotten all pussy whipped.

"I'm gonna take a shower upstairs and grab a few hours' sleep."

Badge heads off upstairs to the rooms above the bar. Anyone can use them as needed, and for Badge it means not having to trek home between shifts.

WILD VALENTINE

I pull out my phone and check the arrival time on the Airbnb sight. Someone called Andreas is arriving in about an hour.

I've been renting out the small cabin on my land for the past few months. I don't need the income, but I like the company every now and again. I wonder what this Andreas is into. I like being there when my guests arrive so I can show them where to go for the good fishing spots, or hunting, or just walking if that's what they're here for.

The sound of heels clacking on tiles gets my attention.

My head jerks up as a vision of loveliness walks in from the back entrance door. She pauses in the doorway and glances about the place with a slight frown on her face.

"Are you guys open for coffee?"

Her voice is as sweet as her countenance. A black skirt clings to her curvy hips, and a ruffled pale green blouse showcases the rise of her large breasts.

She's short and curvy, but her heels give her an extra six inches. They're shiny like she just stepped off a sidewalk in a city instead of wandering into our mountain bar and MC headquarters.

"We don't open for another hour." I've never seen Davis move so fast, but he's over the side of the bar and practically salivating on the counter.

I give him a quick back off scowl.

"But I'm sure we can get you a coffee."

Her eyes dart to mine, and it's like an arrow hits my chest. I suck in my breath as the air rushes out of the room. She holds my gaze in a way that makes my entire body heat.

My heart thunders to a new beat, and one word rings clear in my head.

Mine.

"What would you like?"

Davis's voice breaks the spell, and the angel who just walked into our HQ glances over to him. The loss of her eyes on me feels like a cold wind hitting me in the face.

"Double latte with soy milk." She rattles off her order, and I detect a New York accent. My angel is far away from home, and I'm piqued with curiosity as to what the hell she's doing here. There's no car out front.

"How'd you get here?"

Her gaze shifts back to mine, and I notice the dark shadows under them. There's a little frown creasing her forehead that I long to run my thumb over and smooth out.

"The back door was open," she explains. "My rental car's out back."

She must have driven in the back entrance while

I was talking to Badge.

"I thought you'd be open. It's…" She checks her phone. "After ten."

I chuckle at her confusion. She must be used to getting anything she likes 24-7

"This isn't New York."

Her frown deepens. "How do you know where I'm from?"

My gaze travels lazily up her body from the polished heels to the silk stockings, the tight skirt that restricts movement too much to be any use on a mountain, the carefully ironed blouse with the pretty but useless ruffles on the sleeves and the oversized purse that's not a backpack, which is what most people carry on the mountain.

"Just a lucky guess."

She smiles then, and my breath hitches. My New York angel is even more lovely when she smiles. Her blue eyes light up, and the dark smudges under them seem to fade away.

"Am I over-dressed for the mountain?" she teases.

"Just a little."

Davis hands her a coffee, and she closes her eyes to inhale the scent. As she takes a deep breath she stretches her neck, exposing a pale throat that makes my pulse race. I long to run my tongue up the line of her neck to that sensitive bit the behind the ear.

Christ. What's this woman doing to me? I've known her less than five minutes, and I'm already fantasizing about kissing her throat and ripping that ridiculous skirt off her. I've kept away from women for the last twelve years, and for good reason, but one look at this beauty and all reason goes out the window.

"What brings you to Wild Heart Mountain?"

Her eyes flutter open, and she purses her lips together to blow on the hot coffee.

My cock hardens at the sight of her plump lips, thinking about all the things I'd like her to do with her mouth.

"I'm here for work."

I've got no idea what kind of work could bring a New York angel to this side of the mountain. I'm about to ask when she takes a sip of her coffee and moans.

She fucking moans, a soft little sound that has my cock twitching in my suddenly too tight jeans.

"That's good coffee."

I slide off the stool, because it's too uncomfortable to keep sitting.

Her eyes follow me as I stand up and widen as she takes in my full height. Yup, I'm a big bastard, and next to me my angel seems tiny. She's all short and curvy, and even with the killer heels, I tower above her.

She swallows, and her gaze darts away. It comes to rest on the vintage bike on the wall. She walks over to it and I follow with my eyes, enjoying the way her skirt hugs her ass.

She takes in her surroundings, scrutinizing the pictures on the wall and peering at the inscriptions.

"This is the Wild Riders Motorcycle Club Headquarters."

She states it as fact and I raise my eyebrows, wondering how a girl from New York has heard about our MC.

She leans forward, staring at one of the photos. It's from a Veteran's Day ride and we're straddling our bikes, kitted out in our military gear rather than our MC jackets, ready to hit the road.

"Veterans," she says softly, like she's talking to herself.

"That's right."

She jumps at the sound of my voice, not aware that I had come up behind her. She spins around, and I'm so close that her breasts brush my chest. She lets out a gasp of surprise but doesn't step back.

"Sorry I scared you."

Her eyes are more startling up close. One's deeper blue than the other, but there's no denying the dark smudges underneath. My angel has troubles, and I can't wait to soothe them.

"Why are you here...?"

I don't even know her name. The woman takes a ragged breath, and her lips part. My eyes dart to them, so plump and sweet and agonizingly close.

"Is the coffee alright? I didn't know if you wanted it milkier," Davis calls from the bar. I grit my teeth; the boy's timing is incredibly poor. The spell is broken, and the woman steps back.

"No. Thank you. It's perfect as it is."

She darts back to the bar and retrieves her coffee from the counter. She takes a long sip, determinedly looking forward.

"What's your name?"

I follow her to the bar and lean my elbows against it. Trying to be causal while this woman has me all twisted up inside.

It's been a long time since a woman had me in a spin, and that didn't end well. But I ignore the warning from my brain as my body takes over, making me tongue-tied and hot and hard all at once.

"Hazel," she says.

"Hazel." It's a beautiful name. It suits my angel. "Why are you here, Hazel?"

She sips her coffee and places the mug down slowly.

"I'm looking for someone. Marcus Wild. I heard he's a member of the MC."

My name on her lips makes my chest expand and my cock lengthen. My angel is here for me. How could I be so lucky?

Then it all slides together.

"You're from the magazine."

I push away from the bar as my chest deflates. My angel is here for me, but only to interview me for some goddamn vanity magazine. To exploit my story to sell copies of their pretentious magazine.

She nods. "I'm Hazel Lumley, arts journalist for *Culture Slam* magazine."

She holds out a hand, and I stare at it until she draws it back in. The frown reappears on her face, but this time I'm not so eager to wipe it off.

"I told your boss I'm not interested, so stop harassing me."

Her eyes go wide, and I almost feel sorry for her. "I'm not harassing you…"

Tracking me to the MC headquarters sure feels like harassment to me. "You're kidding, right?"

"Just give me five minutes of your time…"

"Five minutes won't change anything." I hate to do this to, her and I really hope she doesn't lose her job. But there's no way I'm talking to that magazine.

"I'm sorry you've wasted your time, Hazel, but it's a no."

I grab my jacket off the back of the stool and pocket my phone. My guest is turning up soon, and I want to be there to greet him.

A pang of regret tugs at me as I stride past my New York angel. But that's women for you. Duplicitous.

It's best she gets back on the plane and straight home to New York where she belongs.

To keep reading visit:
mybook.to/WRMCWildValentine

BOOKS AND SERIES BY SADIE KING

Wild Heart Mountain

Military Heroes

Wild Riders MC

Mountain Heroes

Temptation

A Runaway Bride for Christmas

A Secret Baby for Christmas

Sunset Coast

Underground Crows MC

Sunset Security

Men of the Sea

Love and Obsession - The Cod Cove Trilogy

His Christmas Obsession

Maple Springs

Small Town Sisters

Candy's Café

All the Single Dads

Men of Maple Mountain

All the Scars we Cannot See

What the Fudge

Fudge and the Firefighter

The Seal's Obsession

His Big Book Stack

For a full list of Sadie King's books check out her website

www.authorsadieking.com

ABOUT THE AUTHOR

Sadie King is a USA Today Best Selling Author of contemporary romance novellas.

She lives in New Zealand with her ex-military husband and raucous young son.

When she's not writing she loves catching waves with her son, running along the beach, and drinking good wine with a book in hand.

Keep in touch when you sign up for her newsletter. You'll snag yourself a free short romance and access to all the bonus content!

authorsadieking.com/bonus-scenes

Printed in Great Britain
by Amazon